I0520187

LYNTON AND THE GHOSTS AT THE MANSION ON BALETE DRIVE

A Retelling of a Classic Tale With A Modern Twist

BY

J. WAYNE FRYE

A NOVELLA

This book is written in Canadian English, so teachers should alert their students to the differences in spelling, based upon country. A teacher's guide which includes chapter outlines, vocabulary and questions is available from the publisher.

LYNTON AND THE GHOSTS
AT THE MANSION ON BALETE DRIVE

TO: Pat Dean Olsen
You gave me more than you will ever know,
as we shared interludes that brought me
comfort in times that were far too fleeting.
You were a grand and glorious part,
for a short time, of a life that is filled
with many fond memories. Thanks for one
of the fondest memories of all.

AND AS ALWAYS, TO MY MUSE
Lynton Viñas

Catalogue Number: 2014-2453579

ISBN: 978-1-928183-18-1

Fireside Books – Victoria, British Columbia
Part of the Peninsula Publishing Consortium

2   **J. Wayne Frye**

LYNTON AND THE GHOSTS
AT THE MANSION ON BALETE DRIVE

TABLE OF CONTENTS

LYNTON AND THE GHOSTS
AT THE MANSION ON BALETE DRIVE

ABOUT THE AUTHOR

The author with the real-life Lynton Viñas

Wayne Frye's *Aaron Adams* mysteries, *Girl* series books and *Lynton* adventures have titillated the brains of those who enjoy tantalizing tales that challenge the mind. His life, like those of the heroes he writes about, has been filled with adventure and excitement.

He has been a college hockey coach, university professor, and at one time, the youngest university president in the USA. Called a marketing genius by the LOS ANGELES TIMES, he has been a promotional consultant to hockey teams and motion picture companies. He has been cited for his work with inner-city gang children in the Los Angeles area and been active in the anti-globalization movement. He became a Canadian citizen in 2003 and lives in Ladysmith, British Columbia and Cavite, Philippines. He provides satirical political commentary to many Canadian newspapers, and his books on politics have created a great deal of controversy.

Some Other Books by J. Wayne Frye

Hockey Mania and the Mystery of Nancy Running Elk
Something Evil in the Darkness at Hopkins House
How Hockey Saved a Jew From the Holocaust
Fighting for Justice in the Land of Hypocrisy
The Girl Who Stirred up the Whirlwind
The Girl Who Motivated Murder Most Foul
The Girl Who Said Goodbye for the Last Time
Fall From Apocalypse
Armageddon Now
Worth
When Jesus Came to Jersey as the Son of Thunder
When Jesus Came to Canada to Lead an Indigenous Rebellion
Canadian Angels of Mercy – Nurses in Times of Peril
Points of Rebellion: Aboriginals Who Fought for Justice
Lynton Walks on Water
Lynton Curls Her Hair
Lynton and the Vampire at Tagaytay Manor
Lynton Buys a Cell-Phone and Hears the Voice of Doom
Lynton and Beowulf in the Taal Inferno
Chablis: Avenging Angel for the Forgotten
In the City of Lost Hope
Chablis and the Terrorist
Pursuit
The Disappearance

J. Wayne Frye

LYNTON AND THE GHOSTS
AT THE MANSION ON BALETE DRIVE

INTRODUCTION
A TINGLING SPINE

Not too long ago, my dear muse, Lynton Viñas, motivated me to emulate my writing hero, Mickey Spillane, and write a book in 24 hours. It was a relatively successful little ditty that managed to make it onto one minor best-seller list. This current book is being written because my muse and I are separated for a few weeks due to our business interests that necessitate us being in two different parts of the world.

As is far too often the case since she lives in the Philippines, today, unable to communicate with her because of a poor internet connection due to a nation that has very little control over corporate internet malfeasance that is as rampant as a fox in a hen house, I have decided to fill the time with a literary sojourn into the world of ghosts and retell, with a modern twist, a tale of ghostly apparitions that may be real or only the result of furtive, imaginative minds of people cast into a situation that created havoc in their lives. So, the best time to read this story will be at night, when you can turn off all the lights save one by your beside, lie back in the semi-darkness and take a journey into the macabre.

Additionally, while formulating this tale in my mind, pleasant memories of a long ago romance flashed into my aging brain that can remember vividly what happened 30 years ago, but has trouble recalling what happened 30 minutes ago. This amazing woman of whom I write, who is as beautiful today as she was all those years ago, maybe even more so, shared many grand interludes with me during my adolescence in which we discussed scary ghost tales. In fact, there was an area between Greensboro and High Point, North Carolina that we would pass which was notorious for a ghost sighting.

J. Wayne Frye

LYNTON AND THE GHOSTS
AT THE MANSION ON BALETE DRIVE

On certain rainy nights, where U.S. 70-A twists around a sweeping curve that passes by an old, overgrown underpass, drivers will see a young woman in a white dress standing by the side of the road, desperately trying to flag down a passing car. If anyone pulls over to help the young lady, she climbs meekly into the back seat of the car and explains that her name is Lydia, and that she has just been to a dance and now she is trying to get home. She gives the driver an address not too far away, and he kindly agrees to take her there.

The driver and/or passenger try to engage her in conversation, but she is always deathly silent, never saying anything after asking to be taken home. Also, there is a sense of deep foreboding eeriness that generally prevails among those who pick her up.

When the car pulls into the address that the young woman gave, the driver turns around to discover that Lydia has vanished. Perplexed and bewildered, the driver goes hurriedly to the door of the house, where a person answers. The man or woman who answers explains in detail what has probably happened, as it has been a somewhat regular occurrence over the years that mystifies one and all.

The person at the door explains that this has happened many times before, usually when it is foggy and raining, as there was a woman who died in a car wreck by that overpass in 1923 during a heavy rain storm. Though her parents have been long dead, apparently the ghost of this girl is unaware of that and is still desperately trying to find her way back into their loving arms. Though the ownership of the home has changed many times over the years, the ghostly visits by the young woman have never ceased, as several times a year motorists pick her up by the overpass and wind up driving her to the place she once called home. However, once there, she has mysteriously disappeared from the back seat of the car, much to chagrin of the startled and dumfounded motorists.

My youthful romance with Pat Dean Olsen was always adventuresome, but each time we drove down that dark, lonely part of High Point Road, both of us would get a tingle up and down our spines. I hope you get the same sensation while reading this book.

LYNTON AND THE GHOSTS AT THE MANSION ON BALETE DRIVE

PROLOGUE
MADE THINGS MORE PERPLEXING

Lynton Viñas was beautiful, but not like those plastic movie stars that parade around in arrogant display of their magnificence or like trophy wives strolling the streets with Gucci packages under their arms. She was beautiful for her inner self that projected a kind heart and a gracefulness of the mind that seemed to sparkle and glow in her captivating smile and penetrating, twinkling eyes. She was beautiful for her ability to bring joy to so many by lifting the spirits of those in pain and making them soar with exhilaration that someone so sweet, so kind and pure could show them compassion. She was not beautiful for something as transitory as looks. She was beautiful deep in her soul.

The renowned Filipino demon fighter sat quietly, listening to the tale being woven by her friend, publisher of the *Manila Herald*, Gordon Sanchez. He had called upon her in the humble abode where she lived in Old Bulihan, in an area of poverty among those who had been discarded by a society that had a gap between the rich and poor every bit as obscene as that found in the USA. In fact, the Philippines had judiciously followed the American model of aggrandizing greed as an enviable trait ever since Marcos had been deposed.

LYNTON AND THE GHOSTS
AT THE MANSION ON BALETE DRIVE

Lynton Viñas was a woman who could afford to live among the rich and famous, but preferred to live as she said, "with the real people." Although her home was a two story villa with a balcony that seemed a bit out of place in the area, everyone was always welcome there to share their burdens and as was so often the case, ask her to intercede for them in their search for justice or to solve perplexing problems involving the supernatural. That was the reason her friend was there on this exceedingly warm humid night.

The story had held her interest, as they sipped lemonade on the second floor balcony sufficiently fascinated as she always was in tales of the supernatural, except the obvious remark that it was an extremely gruesome tale of woe because it involved a child being possessed by some unknown entity or entities.

As he wove his story, Lynton became more interested, as she was never sure she believed in ghosts, but did believe in the power of the mind to manifest things that were conjured up from the dark recesses of the brain where evil often incubated. Yes, this was an interesting case and she listened intently about how a young boy had seemingly been on a slippery slope of sanity that was making his uncle, with whom he and his sister had lived since there mother died when they were infants, so exasperated he had carted the boy off.

J. Wayne Frye

LYNTON AND THE GHOSTS
AT THE MANSION ON BALETE DRIVE

Gordon knew the story through a young reporter who had worked as an administrative assistant with the uncle before coming to the newspaper as a cub reporter. The uncle was looking for a governess/teacher at the present time. It seems one pervious governess had died, and the latest one simply gave notice and did not even stay the two weeks which was customary after doing so. She left the place, refusing to ever sit foot in the house again. The cub reporter, Louis Benificio, had noticed strange things going on in the house, and after being hired by Gordon, he thought it might warrant a story in the Sunday supplement because the place where the parties lived was dark, foreboding and mysterious looking, and the uncle was a man who apparently cared very little for the children, only taking care of them out of a familial sense of duty to his sister whom he looked upon as a pariah, along with her husband, whom she defiantly married despite the objections of a father who vowed to cut her off from any inheritance because of her breach of propriety. To the great delight of the uncle and the father, the husband died in an automobile accident, but unfortunately, the accident also took the life of the daughter.

Before going ahead with the story in the Sunday Supplement, Gordon wanted more details. It seems the reporter had simply disappeared, not showing up for work, and despite a concentrated search, he had apparently vanished without a trace. Now, it was well-documented through books written by Wayne Frye about her exploits, that Lynton was a well-known investigator of the supernatural, particularly any problem involving so-called demons. For that reason, Gordon wanted her to explore the strange goings on in the mansion on Balete Drive, and he wanted Lynton to pose as a teacher/governess in order to explore the supernatural. It had been many months that the master of the state had been looking for a governess, and Lynton, with her beauty and natural instinct for ingratiating herself to people would be a cinch to procure the position.

Now, Lynton was basically not interested, as she had just finished a taxing experience in Tagaytay where a so-called demon had manifested itself in the mind of a young girl, and she had lost a great friend in the battle for the young girl's soul. But Lynton was a young woman with a soft heart that beat with a grand passion for those in dire circumstances, so, she could not help but listen with interest as Gordon continued his tale. When he mentioned that there were two young children that, according to the reporter were possibly in grave danger, she could not help but lend an ear.

Before the evening was over, not really sure why she was doing it, she agreed to apply for the job as a governess, but surely she would have to do it under her real name, as he would run a reference check, and the result would be an unlikely hiring of someone who was so well-known. It was then that Gordon suggested she use the name of her friend Ingrid Bautista, who had been a governess in Japan and Macau. Lynton dialled Ingrid up and broached the subject with her. She heartily gave permission and said she would notify her former employers and assure that the references would be forthcoming. She also told Lynton to let her and their friend, Channa Mendis, know if she needed any help, as they would as always, be there if she needed them. So, thus began one of Lynton's most harrowing adventures.

It must be said that this case, involving an apparition of a dreadful kind in that old house was first brought up when the little boy, sleeping in the room with his mother and waking her up in terror; waking her not to dissipate his dread and soothe him to sleep again, but to encounter also, herself, before she had succeeded in doing so, the same sight that had shaken him. Thus was Lynton's interest titillated even more as she had a keen mind that relished intellectual stimulation, and this story was definitely interesting her more and more.

It is well-known that children are often more perceptive of the supernatural than adults. Perhaps it is the fact that their minds are not yet developed enough to overly-question things with cold calculating logic. That is one reason why the church likes to get young impressionable minds as it is easier to indoctrinate them and exercise greater control that will lead to a lifetime of religious manipulation. The fact the apparent ghost appeared to the boy was understandable in a pristine mind, but the mother had seen it too, and that made things more perplexing.

LYNTON AND THE GHOSTS
AT THE MANSION ON BALETE DRIVE

CHAPTER 1
SOMETHING MORE SINISTER GOING ON

Now, from this point on, I shall tell the story just as Lynton has recorded it, for she meticulously wrote down almost everything that occurred while she was at the house on Balete Drive. She journeyed to the home with trepidation to answer in person the ad for a governess that had already led to a phone call and an invitation to come by and discuss the job. This person greeted her on arrival at the house on Balete Drive, which impressed her as vast and imposing. This prospective patron proved an impeccable gentleman, a bachelor in the prime of life, who cut a dashing figure. He was handsome and bold and pleasant, offhand and actually seemed kind. He struck her, inevitably, as gallant and splendid, but what took her most of all and gave her the courage she afterward showed was that he put the whole thing to her as a kind of favour, an obligation he should gratefully incur. He was obviously rich, possessed expensive habits, and was, no doubt a great charmer of woman. Jonathan Delmonte was a grand charmer of women, as Lynton herself, despite being spoken for by another, could not help but get a flutter at this man's grand and glorious manner. He had this big house as a city residence that was filled with the spoils of travel and the trophies of the chase of many women, whose photos adorned the mantel; but it was to his country home in Palawan, an old family place, that he wished to immediately proceed, leaving her in charge of the Balete Drive estate. These children, by the strangest of chances for a man in his position, weighed very heavily on his hands. It had all been a great worry and, on his own part doubtless, a series of blunders, but he pitied the poor children and had done all he could. People he could find to look after them, as his own servants to were very able. The awkward thing was that they had practically no other relations and that his own affairs took up all his time. He had put them in possession of the home so to speak, which was healthy and secure, and had placed at the head of their little establishment, the head housekeeper, a Ms. Grumman, whom he was sure his visitor would like a great deal. She was actually in charge of the girl child and appeared extremely fond of her. There were plenty of people to help, but of course Lynton, or as he knew her Ingrid, would be the supreme authority in the house. She would also have to look after the small boy with great care as he was very precocious. It seems he had been expelled recently from an exclusive Catholic school for reasons that the master did not care to share. There had been, for the two children, at first a young lady whom they had the misfortune to lose. She had done for them quite beautifully, but she had died, the great awkwardness of which had, precisely, left no alternative but to send the boy to a private school rather than allowing him to, as his sister was, be home-schooled. Ms. Grumman had done as she could for Florence, who was seven while Milton, her brother was 10. In the household was a cook, a housemaid, a chauffeur and an old gardener.

Lynton sighed and asked, "And what did the former governess die of?"

Without any hesitation he barked, "That is not germane to our conversation."

Lynton decided to not push the subject, but rather, look for the answer at another time.

Lynton was an astute observer, and as such, she would carefully and thoughtfully assess the situation. She was young, but not untried, and not nervous. She saw the situation in which she found herself calling for a vision of seriousness with little to alleviate the apparent intense loneliness of the place. Oh, and the foreboding nature of the home seemed to beat heavily upon her as it apparently did all who lived there.

Lynton's extreme attractiveness and obvious professional decorum made Jonathan Delmonte not even bother to check her references. Now, Lynton had actually seen him only twice, but yet he was prepared to entrust the children in her care. He told her frankly all his difficulty in finding a suitable replacement for the dead governess as rumours had swirled about in regards to strange goings-on in the house, things that seemed unnatural. He scoffed at the ridiculousness of it all, and Lynton eagerly nodded her head in agreement.

He made it plain that he was not to be bothered and that all matters must be handled by her without bothering him. She would be assisted by his lawyer, who would see that all necessary monies were made available to her. She had not even been introduced the children, as the master obviously treated them with dispassion.

Lynton, smiling demurely and nodding accommodatingly, readily agreed to the demands so as to access and assess the house and explore its peculiarities. Delmonte reached out and took her right hand and held it with both his hands, thanking her for the sacrifices she was making.

She would remember for many years the whole beginning as a succession of flights and drops, a little seesaw of the right things and the wrong things. After agreeing to meet his appeal, she had at all events a couple of very bad days as she packed things and got ready to move in. She found herself doubtful, felt unsure if tackling this situation was indeed the right thing to do for Gordon Sanchez. In this state of mind she wondered why the children had never been introduced in the presence of Mr. Delmonte. He had just said that they were away visiting the seashore and they would be back in a few days, and Ms. Grumman would, of course, make formal introductions as he could not wait their arrival now that he had procured someone he could rely upon. He had pressing business in Hong Kong, and after that he would be off to Palawan, where he expected to be left in solitude while Lynton handled all matters for him in Manila.

Driving at the noon hour, on a lovely day, along the highway into Manila, Lynton could smell the spring sweetness in the air that seemed to be offering her a coming friendly welcome at the Delmonte estate. Her fortitude mounted afresh but, as she turned onto Balete Drive, she was overwhelmed with a feeling of melancholy. She would remember many times over the years the unpleasant impression she got as she looked down the dark street where the mansion sat all to itself in grand majesty, but all alone in a state of mournful sorrowfulness, far from any prying eyes.

The sun suddenly disappeared behind the clouds and she looked at the stately grey stones of the mansion that appeared to be almost pulsating, almost alive, or were they the pulsating dead, the corpses of lost hope in that place that seemed to have a grey cloud of malcontent hanging over it?

LYNTON AND THE GHOSTS
AT THE MANSION ON BALETE DRIVE

Did they represent the coming dread of a place that, for some reason, was making her shiver in anticipatory fright?

In the deep recesses of her mind, Lynton thought of green valleys and serene mountain streams, as she looked upon this place of melancholy. She wanted to put the dread from her mind, but no matter how hard she fought it was there, playing a symphony of discontent.

I am to dwell in a lonely house I know
That embraced evil many a summer ago,
And left no trace but the cellar walls,
And a cellar in which the daylight falls,
And the evil never ceases to grow.

O'er ruined hopes there is no shield
The dark words encase the mowing field;
The orchard tree has grown stiff like a corpse
Darkness abounds and the light has no source;
The footpaths serve as a ghostly shield.

I am to dwell with a strangely aching heart
In that ghostly abode there far apart
On that disused and forgotten road
Where I now must carry a heavy load.
Night comes; the black bats tumble and dart.

The whippoorwill is coming to shout
And hush and cluck and flutter about:

J. Wayne Frye

LYNTON AND THE GHOSTS
AT THE MANSION ON BALETE DRIVE

I hear him begin far enough away
Full many a time to say his say
Before he arrives to shout it out.

It is under the small, dim, dark star.
I know not who these mute folk are
Who share the unlit place with me-
Those stones out under the low-limbed tree
Doubtless bear names that goodness mar.

Ghosts are tireless folk, but slow and sad,
And I, Lynton, must defend lass and lad,
With none among them that ever sings,
And yet, in view of how many things,
They want all the happiness they had.

I am here to serve and protect,
But I know not the ghost's dialect.
Darkness descends like a mist at night
Shrouding this place of devilry in fright
As the evil is all about, which I can detect.

The demon fighter was supposed to be going after evil ghosts, and she did not even know for sure that they existed. Rumours did not make fact. Lynton was a determined woman, but when she arrived on Balete Drive, she felt dread and could sense the evil lurking there that wanted to capture souls and devour hope. Her little red Isuzu puttered toward the house where something wicked waited.

J. Wayne Frye   21

LYNTON AND THE GHOSTS
AT THE MANSION ON BALETE DRIVE

Many years later she would tell her perceptively astute friend Channa Mendis that the lawn and the bright flowers and the crunch of her wheels on the gravel and the clustered treetops over which the rooks circled and cawed in the grey sky sent chills up and down her spine. The scene had a greatness that made it a different affair from her own modest home, and there immediately appeared at the door as she approached the house with bag in hand, a little girl standing beside a civil person who slightly bowed as if Lynton was a distinguished visitor.

Lynton nicely settled into a room that was almost as large as her entire condo where she lived in Old Bulihan. The large, impressive room, one of the best in the house, the great canopied bed, the gold-braided draperies, the long ornate mirror on the huge walk-in closet like the extraordinary charm of the little girl who had joyfully clung to her since the initial introduction made her foreboding interlude fade.

For awhile, Lynton's disconcertion dissipated as she and little Florence, or as she wanted to be called, Flo, were happily bonding with one another. As well, from the first moment, that Lynton set eyes upon the head housekeeper, Ms. Grumman appeared to adore her. The only thing indeed that in this early outlook might have made her shrink again was the clear circumstance of her

J. Wayne Frye

being so glad to see Lynton to the point it became almost worrisome. She perceived Ms. Grumman a stout, simple, plain, clean, wholesome woman. Still, there was something very reserved about her, something she seemed to be harbouring deep within.

Little Flo appeared to Lynton on the spot a creature so charming as to make it a great fortune to have the privilege to tutor her. She was the most beautiful child Lynton had ever seen, and she afterward wondered why Jonathan Delmonte had not told her more of the child as she was so adorable.

She slept little that night, as she thought over the events that had led her to accept Gordon's investigative invitation. She reflected on the radiant image of the little girl, the vision of whose angelic beauty had probably more than anything else to do with the restlessness that, before morning, made her several times rise and wander about the room to take in the whole picture and prospect; to watch, from her open window, the coming dawn, to look at such portions of the rest of the house as she could observe, and to listen, as the morning birds began to twitter, for the possible recurrence of a sound or two, less natural and not without, but within, that she had fancied she heard. There had been a moment when she believed she recognized, faint and far, the cry of a child; there had been another when she found just a faint hint of someone outside her door. Yet, the sounds were not disturbing enough to make her want to open the door and peer out.

In Lynton's room was a small bed in a far corner that was apparently there for Flo to use if she got scared at night. It had been discussed with Ms. Grumman downstairs that Flo was often scared at night and needed comforting, so the bed was there if and when she became frightened. Apparently, she often had horrible nightmares.

At breakfast, Lynton shared the large dining table with Flo at the far end. She encouraged the girl to move down near her, and she also asked Ms. Grumman to join them rather than eat in the kitchen as was apparently her custom. She seemed shocked and said, "Oh my, I couldn't do that, I am just a servant."

Lynton, used to the Filipino culture, which like that in America, was terribly stratified by social class, replied, "A servant or a bank president makes no difference. You are as worthy as anyone else to sit at this table, and as long as I am given the mistress-ship of this house, any servant may sit at the table with me."

"My goodness, Ms. Viñas, what would the master say?"

LYNTON AND THE GHOSTS
AT THE MANSION ON BALETE DRIVE

"Frankly, I don't care what the master says, and my name is Lynton, please."

Ms. Grumman humbly bowed her head and acquiesced to Lynton's request, going to the kitchen and bringing in her breakfast, then sitting on the opposite side from little Flo.

Lynton said, "And the little boy, does he look like Flo here? Is he too so very remarkable?"

"He is fair, mannerly and very remarkable in every way."

"Then I look forward to seeing him when he arrives from his boarding school. If he is anything like his uncle, he must indeed be a handsome lad."

Smiling, Ms. Grumman said, "Well, the master is indeed a handsome man and his nephew is no less handsome for a little boy. Perhaps it runs in the family."

Lynton said, "And he will be home from school tomorrow?"

"Not tomorrow, Friday, miss. He arrives by a limousine sent to pick him up at Tagaytay. His uncle does not like for him to travel by public transportation as it exposes him to all kinds of germs.

LYNTON AND THE GHOSTS
AT THE MANSION ON BALETE DRIVE

What Lynton felt the next day was nothing that could be fairly called a reaction from the feeling of dread upon her arrival; it was probably at the most only a slight oppression produced by a fuller measure of the scale, as she walked around, gazed about with interest, took the full measure of the place in, and thought of her circumstances.

There was still some trepidation on her part, but she was feeling more at ease. Lessons for Flo were to be ignored at present as she wanted to get better acquainted with her. She reflected that her first duty was, by the gentlest arts she could contrive, to win the child into the sense of knowing her so that she would feel comfortable in sharing anything at all with her. She spent the day with her out-of-doors; she arranged with her, to her great satisfaction, that it should be she, she only, who might show Lynton the place. She showed it step by step and room by room and secret by secret, with droll, delightful, childish talk about it and with the result, in half an hour, of her becoming immense friends with Lynton, who was a master at ingratiating herself to people big and small.

Young as Flo was, Lynton was struck, throughout her little tour, with her confidence and courage with the way, in empty chambers and dull corridors, on crooked staircases, her morning music, her disposition to tell her so many more things than she asked, rang out and led her on. She

J. Wayne Frye

LYNTON AND THE GHOSTS
AT THE MANSION ON BALETE DRIVE

looking back on it many years later realized she should have sensed something forebodingly sinister about the way the little delightful girl was so adult-acting. But as her little conductress, with her hair of glistening darkness and her immaculate attire, danced before her around corners and pattered down passages, she had the view of a mansion of the mind that seemed to make the rollickingly gay little girl an impossible target for any ghostly presence.

Yet, there was something not right about the big, ostentatious house, embodying a few features of a building still older, half-replaced and half-utilized, in which she had the fancy of being almost as lost as a handful of passengers in a great drifting ship. Strangely, Lynton was the captain of the ship now, and it would be she who would have to chart uncharted seas into the minds of the children who apparently were treading between heaven and hell, and what of Ms. Grumman? Ah, it would not do to ask her of the strange goings-on just yet; it would be best to let that lie fallow for awhile.

On Friday morning, Ms. Grumman received a call from the Jeepney Terminal in Alabang. It was Milton, who had been dropped off there by the limo driver. When asked why the driver did not deliver him to the house, he said that the driver simply decided that it was too far, so he dropped him off and gave him 11 pesos to ride home on the

LYNTON AND THE GHOSTS
AT THE MANSION ON BALETE DRIVE

Jeepney.

Appalled that an adult would do that to a young boy, Lynton was furious, but rather than call the limo company, she grabbed Flo and headed toward the terminal to pick him up, telling Ms. Grumman to tell him to wait.

As she started out the door, the postman walked up, handing her the mail which she immediately opened. There was one letter from Jonathan Delmonte and all it said was *I trust you have taken charge by now and shall need no assistance. My confidence in you is complete in regards to Milton's dismissal from school.*

She handed the note to Ms. Grumman who was standing there by the door. As she read it, Lynton said, "What does it mean this dismissal from his school."

She gave her a dumbfounded look; then, visibly, with a quick blankness, said, "But they are all sent home for the Spring Break."

"He was sent back permanently. In other words, he was expelled. I was already told this before."

Bowing her head, Ms. Grumman, in almost a whisper, said, "It is not the first time miss. This is twice now that he has been expelled."

J. Wayne Frye

LYNTON AND THE GHOSTS
AT THE MANSION ON BALETE DRIVE

As little Flo just stood and smiled, almost as if she found it amusing, Lynton said, "You mean he was expelled from another school?"

"Yes miss. I am afraid so."

"Why?"

"That you would have to ask the master, miss. I was not privy to the reason."

Taking Flo by the hand, Lynton walked out with her in tow, and headed for the Jeepney terminal, leaving Ms. Grumman just standing in the doorway dumbfounded.

They made their way to the car, then as they drove to the terminal, Flo expressed in her little way an extraordinary detachment from disagreeable goings-on, looking to Lynton, however, with a great childish light that seemed to offer it as a mere result of the affection she had conceived for her now, which had rendered necessary that she should follow her without question to get Milton.

On the way, Lynton could not resist asking her pointedly if she had ever known Milton to be bad. "Absolutely no," replied Flo with great verve and resolution with a stern countenance that seemed to emphasize her commitment to her brother.

LYNTON AND THE GHOSTS
AT THE MANSION ON BALETE DRIVE

Lynton pulled over to the curb and phoned the limo company and told them what had happened. She was furious, but the owner said, "Ma'am, the little boy hurled invective expletives at the driver. The driver was told by the headmaster of the school to be careful with the boy, not to rile him up as he had a corrupt influence on his schoolmates and had done horrible things. The driver noticed that he was playing with something in the back seat. He pulled over and looked in the back. The boy had a small pen knife and was cutting the seat. He was appalled and told him to stop. I am too much of a gentleman to repeat to a lady what he said. The boy was threatening the driver. The driver did exactly as I would have done. We do not have to put up with abusive behaviour."

Lynton thanked him profusely. She apologized for Milton's behaviour, said she would arrange to pay for any damages and hung up. She sighed, looked over at Flo, who had a sinister smile pursing her lips. There was something very strange going on. Then Flo said, "Milton is like him."

"Like your uncle??"

Flo lowered her head and began to hum. She was not going to answer. Then Lynton said, "Your other governess. Did she like Milton?"

LYNTON AND THE GHOSTS
AT THE MANSION ON BALETE DRIVE

Flo got a far away look in her eyes, almost as if she was in a trance. Action was required. Lynton dialled Ms. Grumman. "Ms. Grumman, I need to ask you something. The governess before me, was she young and pretty?"

"Yes."

"Was she enamoured with the master?"

Confused, Ms. Grumman replied, "Enamoured miss. I don't know what that means?"

"Was she infatuated with him?"

"Well, most women are I suppose, but I saw no indication of it. She was more, well more. It was him" Then she just stopped and went completely silent.

The silence was almost deafening. After a few seconds, Lynton said, "But of whom did you speak first? What do you mean it was him?"

Seemingly discombobulated, Ms. Grumman said, "Oh, the master of course, Mr. Delmonte."

There was obviously no one else Lynton supposed, but yet she held the impression of her having accidentally said more than she meant; and that troubled her. What was she holding back?

LYNTON AND THE GHOSTS
AT THE MANSION ON BALETE DRIVE

"Ms. Grumman, did the former governess have trouble with Milton?"

"If she did, she never told me."

Lynton, very deliberate, said, "Was she a very fastidious person. Was she prone to exactness, and would you say that she and Milton got on well?"

"O.K., I suppose."

"Was there anything strange seeming between she and Milton or Flo?"

"Well, miss, she's gone. I won't tell tales."

"I quite understand your feeling. Did she die at the estate?"

"No, she up and left."

"Why?"

"She just left the house one day, at the end of the school term to go home, as she said, for a short holiday, to which the time she had put in had certainly given her a right. We had then a young woman, a nursemaid who had stayed on and who was a good girl and clever; and she took the children altogether for the interval. But our young lady never came back, and at the very moment I was expecting her I heard from the master that she was dead."

"But of what?"

"Just dead ma'am. But what does this have to do with Milton, miss?"

"I am not sure it has anything to do with it, but he caused much trouble with the limo driver. There are some things going on that are bothering me, and when I return we must converse further."

"Oh miss; he is a good boy, a very good boy. Please do not be too harsh with him."

"I shall not," Lynton said as she hung up. She restarted her engine and they drove to the terminal in silence. Flo was delighted to see Milton and they embraced heartily.

As Milton had his arms around Flo, he was staring intently at Lynton who smiled at him. She introduced herself and vowed to say nothing about the incident at that point. She did, however, say, "I should have your knife please."

Without hesitation, he reached in his pocket and handed to her smiling. Brother and sister got in the back seat together and Lynton drove off, but was constantly glancing in the rear view mirror.

LYNTON AND THE GHOSTS
AT THE MANSION ON BALETE DRIVE

The two of them were whispering extremely low and giggling. Were they just two siblings happy to see one another and sharing giddiness as youths will, or was there something more sinister going on?

J. Wayne Frye

LYNTON AND THE GHOSTS
AT THE MANSION ON BALETE DRIVE

CHAPTER 2
DISAPPEARING INTO THE DARKNESS

Milton and Flo ran off upstairs to the playroom and Lynton sat at the dining room table having tea with Ms. Grumman. They sat in relative silence only exchanging the most cursory of pleasantries.

Milton's problems at school and in the limo were more intimately than ever causing Lynton stupefaction. His actions were so monstrous she was ready to pronounce it that such a child as had now been revealed to her should be under intense scrutiny. Still, she was mildly impressed with the way he had greeted her, wistfully looking out with a great glow of freshness, the same positive fragrance of purity, in which she had, from the first moment, seen his little sister. He was incredibly beautiful for a boy, and Mrs. Grumman had put her finger on it - everything about him spoke of an intensity of spirit and deep rooted intelligence. He had an indescribable little air of knowing nothing in the world but civility with Lynton, so what had caused the trouble at school and in the limo? He seemed incapable of such horrid acts. He had a sweetness about him that begged for acceptance and made you want to hug him. Still, beneath the surface one could feel there was an inner turmoil. It was troubling in someone so young. There was a duality of purpose boiling beneath the surface.

LYNTON AND THE GHOSTS
AT THE MANSION ON BALETE DRIVE

Sighing, she said to Ms. Grumman, "What happened was horrible, grotesque."

"You mean his cruelty."

"Look at him my dear woman. He seems incapable of cruelty, yet I know it is true, due to what he did in that limo today."

Bowing her head slightly, Ms. Grumman said, "Will you reply in regards to the expulsion. Say something to the school?"

"No, I shall not reply at all to the school. Nor will I tell his uncle of today's occurrence."

Again bowing her head, Ms. Grumman said, "And what will happen to little Milton?"

"It is a closed matter. I shall say nothing to him either. We simply move forward."

Then Lynton, beginning to think it was time to broach the subject of ghost tales, said, "Is there anything unusual going on in this house? Anything at all that you might want to share with me, something that might make me better able to serve the interests of the children? You know that there have been rumours about strange goings-on here. Maybe that is having a deleterious influence on the children?"

J. Wayne Frye

LYNTON AND THE GHOSTS
AT THE MANSION ON BALETE DRIVE

Ms. Grumman became stiff, sitting up straighter in the chair. She got a very stoic look on her face and empathically said, "There is nothing."

There is a right time and a wrong time to be more forceful, but Lynton felt this was not the time. All she said was, "You will stand by me in trying to help the children?"

She reached over, placing both her hands on Lynton's right hand that was on the table. She held it firmly. "I shall stand by you yes. I love those children."

Today, Lynton looks back at that time and it reminds her that she should have better understood what was going on, but she was, like so many would have been, captivated by the need to protect the children, and the truth was, the desire to not burden them was perhaps a grave error.

Still, the job had now become more than about trying to get the story for the Sunday Supplement. In fact, she called Gordon Sanchez and said that it would take much longer than expected, but that she was onto something big, and if he felt she was costing him too much money, she would do it for free. He was adamant in stating that he had complete confidence in her and that she was to see it out no matter how long it took. He trusted her implicitly.

LYNTON AND THE GHOSTS
AT THE MANSION ON BALETE DRIVE

She did not tell Gordon that she was overwhelmed with a great wave of consternation and pity. Looking back, she now realizes that she found it simple, in her ignorance, her confusion, and perhaps her conceit, to assume that she could deal with a boy whose education for the world was all on the point of beginning. She is unable even to remember at this day what proposal she framed for the end of his holidays and the resumption of his studies with her as his tutor. Lessons with her, indeed, that spring made Lynton realize that she had, for a time at least found the air and freedom, all the music of the spring and all the mystery of nature surrounding her there on Balete Drive. And then there was the considerable stipend she was earning from the press. She truly was enjoying the children but could not help but wonder if she was falling into a trap, not one of design, but one of deep imagination, to her delicacy, perhaps to her vanity; to whatever in her was most excitable by the seemingly quaint circumstances of, in a sense, being a mother, which she had often dreamed of over the years. She found herself forgetting the reason for being there. The best way to picture it all is to say that she was off guard, which in the circumstance was a huge mistake.

The children gave her so little trouble, because they were of a gentleness quiet extraordinary. She speculated often at how the future might handle two such delicate creatures that seemed to beg for

J. Wayne Frye

LYNTON AND THE GHOSTS
AT THE MANSION ON BALETE DRIVE

love. She feared them being bruised by the reality and harshness of life. They had the bloom of health and happiness; and yet, she sometimes felt like she was holding two grenades in her hands and that any minute the pins might be pulled. There simply was something not right.

This charm of stillness may have been, of course, above all, in reflection less idyllic than imagined, because there came a change that broke into this stillness. It was that hush in which something gathers or crouches. The change was actually like the spring of a beast.

In the first week, the days were long; they often, at their finest, gave Lynton at the end of the day, a small interval alone. Much as she liked the children, this time was the thing in the day she liked most; and she liked it best of all when, as the light faded or rather, the day lingered and the last calls of the last birds sounded, in a flushed sky, from the old trees, she could stroll the grounds and think of her boyfriend, Wayne, who was off on an adventure in Nepal, preparing to climb Mount Everest. She enjoyed, almost with a sense of property that amused and flattered her, the beauty and dignity of the place and wondered why there had been any rumours of ghosts, as she had queried Ms. Grumman indirectly and never received any hint of supernatural occurrences. It was a pleasure at these moments to feel herself tranquil and justified; doubtless, perhaps, also to reflect that by her discretion, her quiet good sense and general high propriety, was giving comfort to two of the sweetest children she had ever known in her 30 years.

What she was doing had earnestly become a labour of love. However, this labour of love was about to take a sinister turn. It was a balmy evening, and in the middle of her stroll, while the children were tucked away, she sensed as she strolled the grounds that someone was watching her from afar. She kept turning around to look but no one was in sight. She meandered off the grounds, walked down to the end of the road and turned, strolling back in an extremely leisurely fashion. The house came into view and the moon was at half face casting an eerie glow on the roof of the home. Below the roof was a long cantilevered balcony that extended along the front of the house for maybe 20 feet. The children were forbidden to play on it for fear they might fall. Anyway, it was on the third floor and they were on the second floor tucked away in their beds. She did not look at the balcony at first, only gazed at the second floor where the children were asleep. Suddenly, her eyes scanned upward and she saw it. What arrested her on the spot, and with a shock much greater than any vision had allowed for was the sense that her imagination had, in a flash, turned upon her. There was a man high up on that balcony, which seemed a grand and glorious stage for a figure so imposing, but there was something else about it. It produced in her, this figure, in the clear twilight, two distinct gasps of emotion, which were, sharply, the shock of her first and that of her second surprise. Her second was a violent perception of the mistake of the first: the man who turned and met her eyes was not the person she had precipitately supposed. There came to her thus a bewilderment of vision of which, after all these years, there is no living view that can to given. An unknown man in a lonely place had her spellbound with fear. This man, this image had a ghostly glow about it, and it did not falter in its gaze upon her. It was as if his eyes were the fires of hell itself. Her body became warm all over, slowly heating up more and more as she was overwhelmed with the evil emanating from this ghostly apparition. Oh, but was it an apparition? She felt that this image had been in her mind before. Was it in a nightmare from long ago, maybe from childhood when she was living on the streets of Manila, a poor waif, and used to experience terrifying dreams and wake up screaming? She stood perfectly mesmerized, unable to move as the house, in the strangest way in the world, had, on this instant, and by the very fact of its appearance, become a solitude totally separated from the rest of the world. It was as if, while she took it all in, all around her seemed to be the melancholy of a scene that had been stricken with death. No flowers were blooming; no nightingales were chirping, no cars were making noises rumbling down the street. There was simply an intense hush in which the sounds of evening dropped and dissipated into deathly silence. Yes, the silence of the grave. The sky, except for the moon was pitch black, and there was no voice given to reason.

There was a stilling of all nature, and indeed she saw everything before her with a stranger sharpness. The humidity and heat faded and there was a chill in the air that quaked to the bone, causing her to shiver. The man who was gazing with intensity at her, who looked at her over the railing of the balcony was as definite as a picture in a frame. That's how she thought, as with extraordinary quickness, she thought of each person that he might have been and that he was not. She was confronted with the intensity of inquisitiveness to ask who then he was and to feel, as an effect of her inability to render an answer the greatest uneasiness she had ever experienced. Her heart was pounding rapidly as she stood transfixed.

It is only natural for the reader to ask how long this must have lasted. Well, despite the detailed disposition here to paint the picture as vividly as possible. The great question, or one of these, is, afterward, with regard to certain matters, the question of how long this situation must have lasted. Well, it was an instant, a quick passing of time as she caught at a dozen possibilities, none of which made a difference for the better, that she could see, in there having been this person in the house, but yet, here he was. How long had a person of whom she had been ignorant been milling about?

Still, as she pondered the question of this visitant, she was tempted to call out to him, but her voice would not come. Were they not too far apart to call to each other, anyway? At a shorter range, some challenge between them, breaking the hush, would have been the right result of their mutually transfixed stare. He was in one of the angles, the one away from the house, very erect, as it struck her, and with both hands on the edge as he leaned over the railing staring intensely.

She, no doubt, saw him as clear as possible in the darkness with the moonbeam glistening. She saw him as clearly as the reader sees the letters form on this page; then, exactly, after a minute, as if to add to the spectacle, he slowly changed his place, passed in a methodical gait by looking at her hard all the while, as he walked to the far corner of the balcony where steps ascended in a spiral manner to the side of the house. She had the sharpest sense that during this transit he never took his eyes from her, and his hand, as he went, passed from one of the knobs on the railings to the other to the next. He stopped at the far corner, but less long, and then as he turned away still markedly fixed upon her as he stepped onto the stairs, descended them slowly disappearing into the darkness.

LYNTON AND THE GHOSTS
AT THE MANSION ON BALETE DRIVE

CHAPTER 3
QUINCY IS DEAD

Lynton stood there mystified and bewildered. She stood and waited, but suddenly realized there was nothing to wait for. She was deeply shaken. Was this a secret at the mansion on Balete Drive to which no one had alluded? Maybe he was a mysterious insane, unmentionable relative kept in unsuspected confinement?

She turned the thought over and over in her mind as she just stood and stared at the emptiness. She walked slowly and methodically through the intense darkness into the house. As she got inside, all the lights were off and the darkness appeared to surround her and close in, wrapping her in its blackness. Agitation seemed to take hold of her as she walked in a circular motion about the place, somewhat overwhelmed by the very strangeness that had manifested itself. Part of the strangeness was, in fact, that in the dark hall, there was Ms. Grumman. There, in the darkness, she was staring at Lynton and she got the impression in the flickering moonlight that was filtering through the window at the top of the staircase where Ms. Grumman stood that she was glad to see Lynton. It came to Lynton straightway, under her contact, that, with plain heartiness, mere relieved anxiety at her appearance, Ms. Grumman knew nothing whatever that could bear upon the incident Lynton

LYNTON AND THE GHOSTS
AT THE MANSION ON BALETE DRIVE

had just experienced. .

Lynton had no desire to frighten Ms. Grumman, as it had become obvious that she was a simple woman who was easily excitable. Today, if you asked Lynton when the real terror started, scarce anything in the whole history of her sojourn at Balete Drive seems to be at odds with the fact that her real beginning of fear was on that night.

On the spot, accordingly, in the darkness and with her eyes on Ms. Grumman, she, for a reason incomprehensible, achieved a peaceful inward resolution to spare this woman any fright. She excused herself, walked up the stairwell and headed for her room. The night passed, but a feeling of a coming calamity did not. There were hours, or at least there were moments, snatched even from clear duties, when Lynton had to shut herself off from others to think. It was not so much yet that she was more nervous than that she could not put the sight of that man on the balcony out of her mind. She pondered and pondered the event and simply could arrive at no account whatever of the visitor with whom she had been so inexplicably and yet, so intimately concerned.

It took little time to see that she would need quiet forms of inquiry without exciting any domestic complications from the help. The shock she had suffered sharpened all her senses; and she

J. Wayne Frye

felt sure, at the end of two days and as the result of mere closer attention, that she had discerned that there were no other people present in the household but those she had met.

Still, of whatever it was that she knew, nothing was known around her by the servants. There was but one sane inference: someone had taken a liberty upon the grounds of the estate. That was what, repeatedly, she thought to herself while sequestered in her room. Yes, the estate had been, subject to an intrusion; some unscrupulous traveler, curious in old houses, had made his way in unobserved, enjoyed the prospect from the best point of view, and then stolen out as he came. If he had given her such a bold hard stare, that was but a part of his indiscretion. The good thing, after all, was that she should surely see no more of him. Yet, she had been sent there to explore the rumours of a ghost that apparently no one there even once entertained the thought of, and, as far as she was concerned, the whole thing was fast appearing to be nothing more than a grand hoax thought up by Louis Benificio to get a job with the *Manila Herald*. Hey, even he had disappeared and could not be found now. Perhaps he knew the truth would expose him as fake and a fraud.

This dilemma did not deter her from tutoring the children, but she knew that her stay there was going to come to an end soon, as she simply saw no indications of any supernatural entities. Yes, she had seen something strange one evening but that was easily explainable.

She was actually enjoying the time with the two lovely children. Being with Milton and Flo was a delight. The attraction of her small charges was a constant joy, leading to her to wonder afresh at the vanity of her original fears, and to better understand the distaste she felt when told of Milton's indiscretions. In fact, she had begun to postulate that Milton was simply a victim of circumstances, as he was as near perfect a boy as she had ever seen.

There was simply nothing sinister going on as far as she could see, and each week she reported to Gordon that she was ready to end the tremendous expenses borne by the paper to keep her there. Still, Gordon insisted that she continue for at least awhile longer just to be sure. Since she was enjoying herself, she did not vehemently protest. She often thought of her Wayne at the end of the day as she sat in the nursery. Then she would reflect on the enjoyment of the classroom where she taught the children and they shared so much joy together. They loved to study fiction and verse; and in so doing, they showed a keen awareness of literature and its inner meanings. Instead of growing used to them, though, she kept making fresh discoveries. There was one direction, assuredly, in which these discoveries stopped: deep obscurity continued to cover the region of the boy's conduct at school. It had been promptly given Lynton, as noted, to face that mystery without any question up to this point. Perhaps even it would be nearer the truth to say that Milton, without a word, he himself had cleared it up. He had made the whole charge absurd. Her conclusion bloomed there with the real rose flush of his innocence: he was only too fine and fair for the little horrid, unclean school world, and he had paid a price for it. Lynton reflected acutely that the sense of such differences, such superiorities of quality, always, on the part of the majority which could include even stupid, sordid headmasters, turn infallibly to the vindictive. Milton was from an aristocratic family but he was as common acting as the waif sleeping on the streets of Manila at night. Yes, it was postulated by Lynton that the boy simply was too common acting, too accommodating to those of a lower socio-economic status. This had made him a pariah at an extremely upper-class school.

Both the children had a gentleness that kept them almost impersonal and certainly quite un-punishable. They were simply beyond reproach when it came to propriety. Lynton felt a special attachment to little Milton, for a reason she could not easily fathom. He was simply this beautiful little boy who was extraordinarily sensitive, yet extraordinarily happy. That, more than in any other quality, made her see him as someone who carried a bright light within him that seemed to always be shining.

He had never for a second indicated any wickedness whatsoever. So, how could he have been expelled from school? She took his kind nature as direct disproof of his having really been engaged in anything inappropriate. If he were wicked, surely she would have seen some indication of it. Had he engaged in any subterfuge Lynton felt she would have caught him at it. She found nothing at all, and he was therefore an angel in her mind. He never spoke of his school, never mentioned a comrade or a master; and Lynton, for her part, never alluded to them. Of course, she was under his spell, and the unusual part is that, even at the time, she perfectly knew she was. But she gave herself up to it; accepted the fact that he was just an incredibly charming boy whom she was growing to love.

There was a Sunday when it rained with such force and for so many hours that all were sequestered in front of the television which was rarely on. The rain happily stopped, and she prepared for a walk with the children, which, through the park and by the road to the local village square, would be a matter of twenty minutes. Coming downstairs to meet Ms.

LYNTON AND THE GHOSTS
AT THE MANSION ON BALETE DRIVE

Grumman in the hall, she remembered Milton's rain coat that had required a bit of sewing to close a tear, which she had done, then placed the jacket on the dining room table. The day was grey, but the afternoon light still lingered, and it enabled her, on crossing the threshold to the dining room, not only to recognize, on a chair near the wide window, then closed, the article she wanted, but to become aware of a person on the other side of the window and looking straight in. One step into the room had sufficed; her vision was instantaneous; it was all there. The person looking straight in was the person who had already appeared to her. He appeared thus again with no greater distinctness, for that was impossible, but with a nearness that represented a forward stride in their intercourse and made her, as she met him, catch her breath and turn cold. He was the same, and seen, this time, as he had been seen before, from the waist up, as the window, in the dining room was on the ground floor, not going down to the terrace on which he stood. His face was close to the glass, yet the effect of this better view was, strangely, only to show her how intense the former had been. He remained but a few seconds, long enough to convince her he also saw and recognized her; but it was as if she had been looking at him for years and had known him always. Something, however, happened this time that had not happened before; his stare into her face, through the glass and across the room, was as deep and hard, but it quitted her for a moment during which she could still watch it, see it fix successively on several other things. On the spot there came to her the added shock of a certitude that it was not for her he was looking. No, no, no, he had come for someone else.

The flash of this knowledge, for it was knowledge in the midst of dread, produced in her the most extraordinary effect, and started as she stood there, a sudden vibration of duty and courage. This was Lynton Viñas, demon fighter, the dynamic dynamo. Still, she felt like neither at that instance. She felt genuinely afraid, and this was a girl renowned for her lack of fear.

Suddenly, that courage returned as she bounded straight out of the door again, reached the door of the house, got, in an instant, upon the drive, and, passing along the terrace as fast as she could rush, turned a corner and came full in sight of where she had seen the peering man. But it was in sight of nothing now, as the visitor had vanished.

She stopped, almost dropping with the real relief that maybe she was seeing things; but she took in the whole scene, blinked her eyes and hoped he would reappear. He did not. She scanned all about the terrace and the whole place, the lawn and the garden beyond it, all she could see of the park, were empty. There were shrubberies and big trees, and she felt with the clear assurance that none of them concealed him. He was there or was not there: not there if she didn't see him. She thought long and hard and asked herself what her friend, the famous transgender private-eye, Chablis Louise Chavez, would do in this situation; then, instinctively, instead of returning as she had come, she went to the window. It was confusedly present to her that she ought to place herself where he had stood. She did so; she applied her face to the pane and looked, as he had looked, into the room. As if, at that moment, to show her exactly what his range had been, Ms. Grumman came into the dining room from the hall. With this she had the full image of a repetition of what had already occurred.

Ms. Grumman saw Lynton as she had seen the other visitant peaking through the window; she pulled up short as Lynton had done. Ms. Grumman turned white, and this made Lynton ask herself if she had been as shocked.

Ms. Grumman stared intensely, and scurried out of the room, and Lynton knew she had then passed out of the house and come round to her and that she should presently meet her. She remained where she was, and while she waited she thought of what she had seen. Then, it occurred to Lynton that Ms. Grumman was genuinely frightened by what she saw. Why? Did she not recognize Lynton? Why would a familiar face peering through a window frighten someone? Yes, why indeed?

She let Lynton know as soon as she came around the corner and loomed into view. "What in the name of goodness is going on?"

She was now flushed and out of breath. Lynton said nothing until she came quite near. "Something strange just happened."

Ms. Grumman said, "You look so concerned? What happened?"

"You saw me peering in the window, but there is more to it than me looking in." Lynton reached out and put her hand to her arm and held it. There was a kind of support in the shy heave of her surprise. "You came here with questions, of course. I have questions too, questions that have been forming in my mind for some time."

"Has anything happened?" said Ms. Grumman.

"Yes. You must know now. Did I appear scared?" replied Lynton.

"Yes, I saw you through the window and you have a quizzical look, but there is a fear to it. I sense something dreadful has happened. Pray tell me what is wrong?"

LYNTON AND THE GHOSTS
AT THE MANSION ON BALETE DRIVE

"Well," Lynton said, "I've been frightened."

Ms. Grumman's manner was almost defensive. Her eyes expressed plainly that she had no wish to be frightened, yet was curious and wanted an explanation. "Then tell me what frightened you?"

"What you saw from the dining room, I also saw, but it was not me I saw, obviously. It was a very evil looking man peering into the dining room. It was as if he was looking intensely for someone."

Ms. Grumman's breathing quickened. "What man was it?"

"As evil looking a man as I have ever seen."

Scanning the area, Ms. Grumman said, "Then where has he gone?"

"I haven't the vaguest idea."

"Have you seen him before?"

"Yes, once before on the front balcony."

She could only look at Lynton bewildered. "Do you mean he's a stranger?"

"Oh, yes. I do not know him."

LYNTON AND THE GHOSTS
AT THE MANSION ON BALETE DRIVE

"Yet you didn't tell me about the other time. Why?"

"No good reason, as I saw no need to alarm you."

"And you saw him on the balcony? Then why would you not have called out to him?"

"I don't know. I suppose I was too mesmerized and shocked."

"So, you have only seen him on the balcony and just recently peering thought that window," she said as she pointed toward the window.

"Yes."

Now, Ms. Grumman was becoming more inquisitive. "And what was he doing on the balcony?"

Suddenly Lynton realized exactly what he was doing, He had been looking in the balcony windows. "My goodness, he was looking in the balcony French doors. There is something he wants in this house."

"Miss, what could he possibly want?"

"I don't in the very least know."

LYNTON AND THE GHOSTS
AT THE MANSION ON BALETE DRIVE

Ms. Grumman said, "You've seen him nowhere but here and on the balcony?"

"Yes."

"How do you know he was looking in through the balcony windows?"

"I don't, as he had turned and was looking down into the front yard when I saw him, but now I know. Now I know he had been looking into the house, looking for something or," then she stopped and got a frightful look on her face, "somebody."

"My or my, how was he dressed?"

"Well dressed I suppose, but casual clothes."

"Should we call the police ma'am? Should we?"

"No, not yet, there is no proof other than the word of a frightened woman." Then, she walked over to the window and looked on the ground that was still moist from previous rain. She looked at Ms. Grumman, and she looked down at the ground, staring intently.

A quizzical look upon her face, Ms. Grumman said, "Should there not be footprints in the moist ground?"

LYNTON AND THE GHOSTS
AT THE MANSION ON BALETE DRIVE

Lynton stepped up to the window and yes, there were footprints alright, but they were obviously hers, based on their diminutive size.

They looked at one another puzzled. Then Ms. Grumman said, "Your description ma'am, can you be more exact and what was his demeanour?"

Lynton took a deep breath. "He was a horror."

"A horror?"

"There was an evil aura about him. It was as if he walked in darkness though the moon was bright. He was maybe six feet, and muscular with a stride that spoke of complete self-confidence and a stern manner. His face was obscured by the dark, but oh his eyes seemed to burn with the fires of hell in them. His stare was disarming and spoke of evil behind that stare, not just normal evil, but evil as an enjoyment. Yes, you could see in his gaze a love of evil."

Now religion exerts a strong influence in the Philippines and exercises great control over government and the people, particularly the poor. Ms. Grumman was a devout believer and poor, so she naturally was a stern adherent to the ideas of the devil playing his mischief, but still she had seen no first hand evidence of this evil man, so she was indeed still sceptical.

LYNTON AND THE GHOSTS
AT THE MANSION ON BALETE DRIVE

Ms. Grumman looked around once more; she fixed her eyes on the duskier distance, then, pulling herself together, turned to Lynton with abrupt inconsequence. "It's time we should be tending to the children. The fright seems to have past do you not think?"

Lynton, very determined, said, "No, it has not passed. There is something evil lurking about here. We must keep a keen eye on the children. Do you understand?"

With a look of bewilderment, Ms. Grumman replied, "Yes ma'am. Yes, I certainly understand, completely." However, her look was one of questioning, as if she doubted that Lynton had seen anything at all. She then offered an observation. "There are rumours about this house I know, but they are just that, only rumours. Perhaps your mind is playing tricks on you?"

Lynton realized that Ms. Grumman was not sure how much reliance she should put on Lynton's story of a man lurking about. She elected to not press the matter, but she did say, "Heed my words, we must keep a close eye on the children."

"You are afraid for them?"

"Yes, and I am frightfully afraid of him. That man is evil."

LYNTON AND THE GHOSTS
AT THE MANSION ON BALETE DRIVE

Ms. Grumman's tired, deeply wrinkled large face showed Lynton, for the first time, the faraway faint glimmer of a consciousness more acute that somehow made out in it the delayed dawn of an idea. She was sceptical, but curious. She said, "What day was it you saw this man on the balcony?"

Without hesitation, Lynton replied, "It was Wednesday. Actually about this same time, around 8:00 PM."

"It was dark then?"

"Yes, but the moon was bright that night."

"But Ma'am, how could he get in. We have a 12 foot fence around the property, thick bushes and a locked gate?"

Lynton, a look of concern on her face, said, "And how did he get out? Or did he?"

Trying to introduce a bit of levity, Ms. Grumman said, "We need to ask him how he got in and out the next time he appears."

"Good idea," said a smiling Lynton. "I will do that next time I see him peering in a window."

Smiling also, Ms. Grumman replied, "Yes."

J. Wayne Frye

LYNTON AND THE GHOSTS
AT THE MANSION ON BALETE DRIVE

Lynton told her to take the kids on their walk and that she would stay there, survey the grounds and see if there was any hint that he might be about. Ms. Grumman nodded affirmatively.

"I am fearful for you miss," said Ms. Grumman.

Smiling confidently, Lynton replied, "Don't be afraid for me, be afraid for that abominable creature whoever or whatever it is. I am tough."

Almost laughing, Ms. Grumman said, "Yes ma'am."

Ms. Grumman turned to leave, walked a few feet and then she halted. She turned around and very seriously asked, "Do you fear for them?" And as she said it, she walked back to the window and peered in.

Lynton walked up, placed her hand on Ms. Grumman's shoulder and said, "You fear for them, too. You are a good woman."

Still peering in the window, she said, "How long was he here?"

"He stood there until I came out. When I arrived here, he was gone."

Sighing Ms, Grumman said, "You are brave."

LYNTON AND THE GHOSTS
AT THE MANSION ON BALETE DRIVE

"No really."

"Oh yes ma'am. I would have been too afraid to come out and face him."

"Neither could I!" Lynton laughed again. "But I did come, because I care for the children."

"Surely, you can better describe him to me."

"How do you describe somebody who is like nobody you have ever seen before?"

"Like nobody?"

"Well," Lynton now giving more thought to the man she saw, offered a further explanation of his looks. "He was a Filipino, but maybe of mixed blood. Yes, definitely mixed as he was not very dark, and his hair, though dark black had a tinge of red in it, and, of course, he was very tall for a Filipino. The hair was close-cropped, almost down to the scalp. He had whisker stubble, but the kind that was, no doubt, the result of simply shaving in such a way as to preserve it. His eyebrows were, somehow, very dark; they looked particularly arched, almost like a devil's horns. His eyes were sharp, strange, awfully strange in that they seemed to have fire in them; but rather small and very fixed. His mouth was wide and his lips thin, and except for his little whiskers he was quite clean-shaven. He gives me a sort of sense of looking like an actor. In fact, he was very handsome in a rugged sort of way."

"An actor," replied Ms. Grumman. "Well, he certainly has put a scare into us, so if he is acting like a devil, he is doing a good job."

"He's tall, arrogant even in his strides." She continued, "He seems to have complete control of his environment and you can see an evil all about him."

"Oh my, oh my, miss."

"You recognize his description?"

She visibly tried to get hold of herself. She placed both her hands on the window sill to steady herself as she was shaking violently and just stood there for a few seconds.

"Would you say he was handsome – very handsome?"

"Yes, definitely."

"And how was he dressed more specifically?"

"Bluish shirt, button-down collar and brown slacks. Not sure of they were shorts or not."

LYNTON AND THE GHOSTS
AT THE MANSION ON BALETE DRIVE

"I know the clothes, but they are the master's clothes."

"So, you do know of whom I am speaking?"

You could see the terror in her face. "Quincy."

"Quincy?"

"Paul Quincy. He was the master's valet, his personal assistant."

Then you do indeed know him?"

"Oh ma'am, yes. He would wear Mr. Delmonte's clothes often when the master was away. He was very brazen about it and much loved that outfit you described. It was more his than the masters. You know that most of the time when Mr. Delmonte was gone it was Quincy who ran things around here in his absence. He enjoyed being left alone here to run things.

"Alone?"

"Yes, left alone here with us."

"You saying he ran the place in Mr. Delmonte's absence."

"Oh yes, run things he did."

LYNTON AND THE GHOSTS
AT THE MANSION ON BALETE DRIVE

The night was well upon the place by now, and the clouds covered the moon, making the darkness seem to wrap itself around the two women and bring a certain feeling of dread. Ms. Grumman had a look of fright on her face and was breathing heavily, and seemed unable to form words that were stuck in her mind but simply would not come out.

Lynton looked about as she waited for a further explanation, but as she prepared to ask her next question, a genuine chill seemed to permeate the air. Leaves rustled in the trees and there were intervals when the wind would whip up and flutter all about them.

The humid, moist air raped the back of the women's necks as wailing, sepulchral, menacing sounds could be heard in the distance as dogs began to bay as if something evil there way was coming. Looking desperately into Ms. Grumman's eyes, Lynton said, "Tell me my dear. Tell me what became of the man Quincy?"

"He, he is no longer around miss."

"Where did he go?"

"Oh miss."

Insistently, Lynton said, "Where did he go?"

J. Wayne Frye   65

LYNTON AND THE GHOSTS
AT THE MANSION ON BALETE DRIVE

"He, he is dead miss."

Those words seemed to reverberate in Lynton's head and that chill in the air became more intense.

"Dead?"

. "Yes. Mr. Quincy is dead."

LYNTON AND THE GHOSTS
AT THE MANSION ON BALETE DRIVE

CHAPTER 4
MALEVOLENT PRESENCE

It was that night that placed the two women in consort in regards to what was happening. Make no mistake about Lynton. She had dealt with unexplainable events over the years as she developed her reputation as a demon fighter and a woman skilled at exposing charlatans. She was not sure that what she saw was a ghost. However, it was obvious that if he was not a ghost he was certainly the spitting image of the former valet and personal assistant, Paul Quincy.

The deeply concerned Ms. Grumman was possessed of half consternation and half compassion in regards to what had occurred. There had been, that evening, no walk taken after the revelation of events, for they simply sat in the living room contemplating what had occurred. After awhile, they retreated together to the study which doubled as a classroom for the children. It was isolated and away from the other servants. They needed to have everything out as a simple way to reduce the situation to the last rigour of its elements. Ms. Grumman, herself, had seen nothing, not the shadow of a shadow, and nobody in the house but Lynton had peered into his eyes. Yet, Ms. Grumman accepted without directly impugning her sanity the truth as it was given to her, and ended by showing Lynton, on this ground, an awestricken tenderness, an expression of the sense of non-questionable privilege, of which the very breath indicated the sweetest of human charities in sympathizing with Lynton's plight having come face-to-face with what was, no doubt, in Ms. Grumman's mind, a spirit.

What was settled between them, accordingly, that night, was that they thought they might bear things together; and Lynton was not even sure that, in spite of her exemption, it was she who had the greatest of the burden. She knew at that hour, she thought, as well as she knew later, what she was capable of doing to shelter the children; but it took her some time to be wholly sure of what her honest ally was prepared for to keep terms with so compromising a situation.

It was gratifying to have Ms. Grumman by her side. For a second, Lynton had considered calling her friends Channa and Ingrid, but they were on vacation together in Singapore and not due back for two weeks. So, she sat at one of the students' desks along side Ms. Grumman who pulled up a straight back chair. They began to trace over what they went through to see how much common ground they must have found in the one idea that, by good fortune, could steady their nerves. It was the idea, the second movement, which led Lynton straight out of the inner chamber of her dread. Perfect in harmony of intent, they vowed to get to the bottom of the strange occurrence while keeping the children free from harm and any knowledge of what happened.

They went over and over every feature of what Lynton had seen. Ms. Grumman said, "He was looking for someone else, you say, someone who was not you?"

Then it struck Lynton like a bolt of lightning. She almost shouted, "He was looking for Milton! Yes, he was looking for Milton."

"But how do you know?"

"I know. Don't ask me how, for I do not know that, but I do know he was looking for Milton. Yes, he was definitely looking for Milton."

"Why?"

"That I do not know, but I tell you he was looking for Milton."

"And what would have happened if he had seen him, miss?"

"I do not know that either. All I can say is that he was scanning the room, looking, looking so intently, and his gaze was downward, not upward. So, he was looking for someone short."

LYNTON AND THE GHOSTS
AT THE MANSION ON BALETE DRIVE

O.K., but why not little Florence?"

"Again, that I cannot answer, but I just know it is Milton he seeks."

"Maybe he wants to find them both?"

"Perhaps you are right, but I just sense that his primary objective is Milton."

"Oh my, they are in danger then - Milton for sure and maybe Flo."

"Yes, I believe Milton for sure and maybe Flo. But perhaps whatever it is can be kept at bay. I have an absolute certainty that if I should see again what I have already seen, I shall offer myself as the sole subject of such experience, by accepting, by inviting, by surmounting it all, I should serve as an expiatory victim and guard the tranquility of the children."

"My miss, it can be dangerous to take on an entity, as I am sure its intentions are indeed evil."

"Ms. Grumman, have the children ever mentioned seeing any entity about, seeing someone unusual?"

"No, absolutely never have they mentioned anything at all about an entity."

J. Wayne Frye

LYNTON AND THE GHOSTS
AT THE MANSION ON BALETE DRIVE

"The children were aware of him though? Aware that he was their uncle's valet?"

Ms. Grumman took a deep breath. "Well, Milton was here yes and would interact with him, but Flo was just a baby, a tiny thing who was taken care of by me mostly, free of any interaction with Mr. Quincy."

"They know of his death?"

"Milton yes. Maybe Flo does, but she was so young."

"Ms. Grumman, this is very important. What were the circumstances of his death?"

Ms. Grumman bowed her head and sighed. "They, they are not pleasant."

"Don't be afraid. Don't hold anything back."

"Well, I suppose it is odd that Milton never speaks of him, almost as if Quincy never existed."

"The circumstances Ms. Grumman, please."

"Well, Quincy and Milton were grand friends. Milton idolized him, and was always hanging around him, and you could often see Quincy whispering things to him."

LYNTON AND THE GHOSTS
AT THE MANSION ON BALETE DRIVE

"So, they were together a lot?"

"Yes, but it was Quincy's doing. I mean he spoiled him. He would often take him off to the garden shed where they would build things together – kites. You know things like that."

"Did he seem a corrupting influence?"

"Oh miss. Quincy was truly corrupt with everyone. I am afraid he was not a very good man at all."

"Yes, one can see the corruptness of soul in his face, especially in his eyes. And what of the rest of the staff? Were they influenced by Quincy?"

"Ma'am, I do no like to speak ill of those with whom I work."

Realizing that Ms. Grumman had actually answered the question by omission, Lynton did not pursue it further. She forbore, for the moment, to analyze this description further than by the reflection that a part of it applied to several of the members of the household, who were still of a small colony. But there was everything to indicate apprehension. Then, Lynton put Ms. Grumman, to the test. It was when, at midnight, she had her hand on the schoolroom door to take leave. Lynton said, "I have it from you then, for it's of great importance—that he was definitely and admittedly a horrible man who sought to corrupt almost all with whom he came in contact?"

"Yes, very much so."

"Why would you not tell Mr. Delmonte about his bad influence?"

"Mr. Delmonte don't like tale-bearing. He hates complaints. He is terribly short with anything of that kind, and if people are all right to him that is all that matters, and Quincy was always respectful of him, but I saw through it – saw that Quincy was just playing him, manipulating him."

"I can understand, because that squares well enough with my impressions of Mr. Delmonte. He is obviously not a trouble-loving gentleman, nor so very particular perhaps about some of the company he keeps. But why would you not broach the subject. My guess is you were afraid of Quincy."

She bowed her head as she said, "I should have told. Yes, I should have, but I was afraid, am still afraid of Quincy."

Lynton placed her right hand on Ms. Grumman's left arm and said, "Why were you afraid of him?"

LYNTON AND THE GHOSTS
AT THE MANSION ON BALETE DRIVE

"Ma'am, please?"

"Did you not fear his effect on little Milton?"

"His effect?" she repeated with a face of anguish and waiting.

"Yes, his effect on innocent little precious lives. They were in your charge."

"No, they were not in mine!" she roundly and distressfully returned. "The master believed in him and placed him here because he was supposed to look after everything. I simply would have been scorned, maybe fired had I questioned Quincy's position."

"So, you stood by and just watched Quincy's corrupting influence?"

She started crying. "No miss, I could not bear it, but what can a poor person do? I am uneducated, can barely read or write. Where can I go? What else can I do?"

Lynton felt bad for pressing her so, because she, herself, had known the sting of poverty when she was young. The church said be fruitful and multiply and her poor parents followed the edicts of the church without giving any thought to the fact they were condemning their children to a life of poverty. The church wanted people to never commit the sin of birth control, but the church did nothing to help those it insisted be born with food, shelter, education, healthcare and a job. Ms. Grumman was just one of the millions of poor who were simply born to serve the entitled classes. Lynton smiled and said, "I am sorry. I should have been more considerate of your situation. Get some rest and we shall talk more tomorrow."

The next day Lynton did not let the children out of her sight. A rigid control was to follow them; yet how often and how passionately Lynton turned over in her mind what she had seen and the fear for the children overwhelmed her.

She called Gordon Sanchez and informed him, without going into detail that things were happening that might well lead to an exciting story for the Sunday Supplement. He encouraged her to stay on and report when appropriate.

Lynton lay down after putting the children to bed and simply mulled over all that had occurred. As much as she had discussed with Ms. Grumman, she was, in the immediate later hours still haunted with the shadow of something Ms. Grumman had not told her. Lynton had kept back nothing, but there was a word Mrs. Grumman had kept back. She was sure, moreover, by morning, that this was not from a failure of frankness, but because on every side there were fears. It seems to her today, in retrospect, that by the time the sun was high she had restlessly read into the facts before her almost all the meaning they were to receive from subsequent and crueler occurrences. What she had been given above all was just the terribly sinister figure of the living man. Though he was dead now, perhaps his evil was living long after his demise.

The next day, Lynton finally got the details of Quincy's death from Ms. Grumman. One dawn of a summer's morning, Quincy was found, by a labourer going to early work, stone dead on the entryway to Balete Drive right past the guard-posts. It was explained, superficially at least, by a visible wound to his head; such a wound as might have been produced by a hammer that was apparently used first on his knee, and then, as he bent over in pain, the fatal blow was delivered to the back of his head. There was a cursory investigation, but nothing came of it and the evidence was so scant there was little hope of ever finding the culprit.

It was the opinion of the police, based upon the fact he had extremely high levels of alcohol in his system, that perhaps he had an argument with a drinking buddy who was accompanying him home. How or why someone would be carrying a hammer was simply unfathomable and after

J. Wayne Frye

LYNTON AND THE GHOSTS
AT THE MANSION ON BALETE DRIVE

tracing his steps it was discovered that all the people who knew him had airtight alibis. The inquest and boundless chatter indicated there had been matters in his life, strange passages and perils, secret disorders, vices more than suspected that would have accounted for a number of reasons someone might have hastened his demise.

Now, it is here difficult to put into words what shall be a credible picture of Lynton's state of mind; but it was in the days that followed she was able to dedicate herself to protecting the children from harm. She saw that she had been asked to investigate the strange occurrences rumoured at the Balete Drive home, but now it was more than turning up ghost tales. It was about protecting two of the loveliest children she had ever known.

Many a woman would have fled in horror, but this was the dynamic dynamo, the demon fighter who had faced adversity head on many times and come out triumphant. Thus was a woman who saw the need to stand against evil pure and simple. She was there to protect and defend the little creatures in the world, the most bereaved and the most lovable, the appeal of whose helplessness had suddenly become only too explicit, a deep, constant ache of one's own committed heart. In effect, they were cut off, really, together; but were united in mutual danger. They had nothing but her, as the uncle was too unfeeling, and frankly, Ms.

LYNTON AND THE GHOSTS
AT THE MANSION ON BALETE DRIVE

Grumman simply lacked the innate intelligence to take on such a Herculean task.

In a way it was a magnificent chance. This chance presented itself to Lynton in image rich material. It was as if she would be a screen, between them and the evil that was after them. Well, at least after Milton, but who knows Lynton's thought, little Flo could also be at risk. She considered that the more she saw, the less they would be in danger. She began to watch them in a stifled suspense, a disguised excitement that might well, had it continued too long, have turned to something like madness. What saved her, as one can now see, was that it turned to something else altogether. It didn't last as suspense. It was superseded by horrible proofs, proofs of a malevolent presence that was descending upon that house on Balete Drive.

J. Wayne Frye

CHAPTER 5
EVIL FESTERING AND GROWING

In the afternoon, Lynton was strolling through the grounds with the younger of her charges. They had left Milton indoors, reclining on the sofa by the study window, as he had wished to finish a book, and Lynton had been glad to encourage a purpose so laudable in a young man whose only defect was an occasional excess restlessness. His sister, on the contrary, had been alert to come out, and she strolled with her half an hour, seeking the shade, for the sun was still high and the day exceptionally warm. Although they were together, they both seemed to be given to their own thoughts as the afternoon wore on. The grounds were extensive and they walked awhile then sit awhile, only to rise and walk some more.

The children spent much time together, and they were prone to whisper in the corners of rooms, as most children are given to playful antics they do not want adults privy to in their little worlds. Sometimes Lynton wondered what they were whispering, as when she would approach the whispers would stop and silence would prevail. Lynton's attention to them all really went to seeing them amuse themselves immensely without her. This was a spectacle they seemed actively to prepare and that engaged her as an active admirer. She often agreed to walk in a world of their invention, so that her time was taken only with being, for them, some remarkable person or thing that the game of the moment required and that was merely, thanks to her superior and exalted status in the hierarchy, something they seemingly appreciated from someone who did not have to take such a keen interest in all their endeavours.

The two of them were by the edge of the large pond on the estate. They sat under the gazebo as the sun dipped behind a cloud and a slight drizzle began to fall. Looking across the lake as Flo played with some tiny pebbles that had been laid on the bench upon which they sat; Lynton became aware they had an interested spectator. The way this knowledge gathered in her was strange in which it quickly merged itself. She had sat down to take in with certitude, and yet without direct vision, the presence, at a distance, of a third person. The old trees and the thick shrubbery, made a great and pleasant shade, but it was all suffused with the brightness of the hot, still hour as the rain lightly fell around them. There was no ambiguity in anything; none whatever, at least, in the conviction she from one moment to another found herself forming as to what she saw straight before her and across the lake as a consequence of raising her eyes. They were attached at that point to watching Flo play the pebbles, and she did not move at all while steadying herself as to be able to make up her mind what to do about the strange figure across the pond watching them. This was an alien object; as a figure had no right to be there on the estate.

She counted over perfectly the possibilities, reminding herself that nothing was more natural, for instance, then the appearance of one of the men about the place, or even of a messenger, a postman, or a tradesman from the village. That reminder had little effect on her practical certitude as she was conscious, still now even without looking, of the figure across the way staring intently at them.

Of the positive identity of the apparition she would assure herself as soon as her courage was fortified; meanwhile, with a sharp effort she transferred her eyes straight to little Flo, who, at the moment, had meandered to the back of the gazebo. Her heart had stood still for an instant with the wonder and terror of the question whether she too would see; and Lynton held her breath while she waited for a cry of fear from her when she gazed upon the unearthly apparition in the distance as the rain suddenly stopped.

Lynton waited, realizing that if she were to move too quickly Flo might be mortified by the apparition across the way. She was surprised by a sense that, within a second, all sounds from her had dropped; and, by the circumstance that, also within another second, she had, in her play, turned her back to the water. She asked herself if Flo had seen it and was just indifferent.

Flo had picked up a small flat piece of wood, which happened to have in it a little hole that had evidently suggested to her the idea of sticking in another fragment that might figure as a mast and make the thing a boat. This second morsel, as Lynton watched her, she was very markedly and intently attempting to tighten in its place. Lynton's apprehension of what she was doing sustained her so that after some seconds she felt she was ready to defiantly face that apparition. As she prepared to do so, Flo walked to the edge of the pond and placed the boat in the water, looked up and without any fright whatsoever gazed over at the entity. She did not waver in her countenance, simply continuing to play with the boat as if nothing was there.

Lynton blinked her eyes, and as quickly as the apparition had appeared it was gone. Lynton asked herself if it had really been there. She did not want to ask Flo, but had to know if she had seen it, for surely she had. All she asked her was, "It is lovely across the way when it is raining don't you think, so peaceful across the way."

The little one, without hesitation said, with no indication of having seen the apparition, "Yes."

LYNTON AND THE GHOSTS
AT THE MANSION ON BALETE DRIVE

"Yes, the far side of the pond is so peaceful looking."

Again, a one word reply, "Yes."

She had seen it, of that there was no doubt, but why did she not acknowledge it. There was a distinct apparition of a woman wrapped in a shawl. Lynton decided not to press the issue. Flo, for some unknown reason, did not want to acknowledge having seen the entity.

Returning to the house, immediately upon entering, little Flo frolicked over to Milton and they began that infernal whispering. Standing in the doorway, Lynton was mesmerized by the stare from Milton as he looked her way. His eyes were intense and his breathing was steady and measured. She felt uneasiness, almost as if, for the first time, he might harbour ill intent toward her.

She turned and went into the kitchen, pulling Ms. Grumman by the hand into the dining room. They sat at the table and Lynton said, "They know. It is too monstrous to comprehend, but those two know."

"What miss. What do they know?"

"All that we know. They know about everything. They do. Only a few minutes ago, out by the pond

LYNTON AND THE GHOSTS
AT THE MANSION ON BALETE DRIVE

Flo saw.

"What miss?"

"A different entity this time, there was a woman across the far side of the pond, and Flo looked directly at her, but never admitted to seeing her. She looked directly at her and said not a word."

"Then how miss do you know she saw?"

"I saw it as clear as I see you now, and Flo stood by the pond's edge looking up at the very spot where the woman in the shawl stood. She saw her without question, and upon her return she went over and whispered something to Milton, and he knows too. He knows I tell you."

"Let me get this straight. Now there is a woman who is appearing?"

"Yes, a figure of quite unmistakable horror and evil: a woman in black, pale and dreadful—with such an air also, and such a face! She stood in haughtiness on the other side of the lake. I was there with the child, quiet for a long time and in the midst of it she came."

"Came how—from where?"

"She just appeared and stood there."

LYNTON AND THE GHOSTS
AT THE MANSION ON BALETE DRIVE

"She never approached you?"

"Oh, for the effect and the feeling, she might have been as close as you are to me now. I could feel the hot breath of hell from her though she was across the pond."

Impulsively, Ms. Grumman said, "Was she someone you've never seen?"

"No, never seen her, but Flo has. I just know it."

"Oh my."

"This is important Ms. Grumman. The lady who was their governess before; how did she die?"

"Ms. James?"

"Was that her name?"

"Yes ma'am, but I, I…"

"Was she tall for a Filipino woman, maybe 5:6 or 5:7?"

"Yes."

"Did she have broad shoulders for a woman?"

"Yes."

LYNTON AND THE GHOSTS
AT THE MANSION ON BALETE DRIVE

"Long straight black hair that hung over her shoulders?"

"Yes."

"And did she have a curvaceous body with very pronounced hips and a thin waist?

"Yes ma'am. Are you saying what you saw was Ms. James? My or my, maybe I should ask Flo."

"No, absolutely not. Do not bring the subject up to her. She will lie about it, because she acted as if no one was there. She, for some reason, does not want to admit in front of me that this abomination was there. There is a deep dark secret these children are harbouring."

"But ma'am, what secret could those two little lambs be hiding? My, they are just innocent children."

"Flo doesn't want me to know."

"It's only then to spare you from concern?"

"No. The more I go over it, the more I see in it, and the more I see in it, the more I fear. I don't know yet how to handle this whole affair."

"You mean you're afraid of seeing her again?"

LYNTON AND THE GHOSTS
AT THE MANSION ON BALETE DRIVE

"It is not seeing her I fear. I fear the reasons why the children will not acknowledge seeing the two of them, for I fear they have seen Quincy, too."

You could see the concern weighing heavily on Ms. Grumman. She eased back in her chair dumbfounded and said, "Do you feel she likes this abomination? That she is somehow under its spell?"

"Like the thing? I do not know whether it is like or simply under a spell."

"She is such an innocent little girl."

"Yes, and we must cling to that notion. Still, there seems to be something sinister going on. The constant whispering between the two is bothersome. There is something they are hiding."

Ms. Grumman at this revelation, fixed her eyes a minute on the floor; then at last raising them, "Tell me how you know this thing has evil intentions?"

"You can feel it. There is a chill comes over you and those eyes bore into your soul. She shows every bit as much evil as that thing I saw peering through the dining room window and walking on the balcony. I have fought evil many times, and I know it when I see it. Yet, she never gazed directly at me, only the child."

LYNTON AND THE GHOSTS
AT THE MANSION ON BALETE DRIVE

"Oh my, Ms. James. Ms. James, oh my, oh my."

"I have never seen such wickedness in the eyes as I have seen in the eyes of those two apparitions. She gave no glance my way, only looked at the child, but I could see the wickedness in those stares of damnation."

"Her wickedness was all aimed at Flo?"

"Yes. She never really looked at me. It was as if I was not there."

"You saw in her eyes dislike for little Flo?"

"It was something much worse."

"What do you mean, miss?"

"There was a determination in her eyes, a will so strong that it was as if neither heaven nor hell could stand in the way of her purpose. There was such a fury of intention."

Ms. Grumman was as white as a sheet now. "Intention?"

"Oh, I can see her intention. It is carved into those eyes, and what is worse, Flo also knows her intention and seems to embrace it."

LYNTON AND THE GHOSTS
AT THE MANSION ON BALETE DRIVE

Ms. Grumman was now so nervous she could not sit still. She got up and began to walk about the room. She stood by Lynton, looked down and said, "Was she in black?"

"Yes, it was almost as if she was mourning."

"Was she a fine looking woman?"

"Yes, very attractive. And, how could I put this? Well, she was very alluring looking. There was a strong sexual element to the way she stood there. Yes, she was an alluring woman, very alluring. However, she was much more. She was sinister-looking."

"Ms. James was alluring, very alluring, very sexual, but brazen. Yes, so brazen. I never brought it up, because I didn't want to speak out of turn."

"Oh my." Lynton stood, placed her hands on Ms. Grumman's shoulders and looked directly in her eyes. "This is critical. How did she die? Of what did she die? Tell me direct. There was something between her and Quincy, right?"

"Oh miss, there was everything between them, everything. She was a lady when she came here, but she lusted after him so. Oh, she was always staring at him, and he at her. It was disgusting to watch them pine for one another."

LYNTON AND THE GHOSTS
AT THE MANSION ON BALETE DRIVE

Lynton felt that she doubtlessly needn't press too hard for details, but she could not resist saying, "They were so brazen as to show sexual attraction in front of the children?"

"They did ma'am. It was horrible, and I wanted to tell the master, but Quincy told me to keep my mouth shut or he would do something that would get me fired, because he had the master's ear. He was that way with all women miss. He had many others who fell for his lascivious nature. Oh, he had no shame. He did exactly as he wished with one and all, especially with Ms. James."

"Did Ms. James know about his infidelity with other women?"

"She did, but she was so fascinated with him, so under his spell she had no pride. In the end she paid for her lust though."

Lynton let go of her shoulders, sat back down and looked up at her. "What Ms. Grumman did she die of?"

Just then Flo and Milton came running in, and Lynton stopped her questioning, not wanting to alarm the children. However, her alarm did not recede. The children were lost. Yes, they were lost to an evil that was festering and growing. She felt helpless.

J. Wayne Frye

CHAPTER 6
BATTLE THE DARKNESS

I am sitting her with visions of you dancing in my head darling. I can feel the warmth of your smile. I can see those twinkling dark eyes. I can smell your freshness. I carry your love with me like a treasure locked away safely in my heart. Each breath I take bristles with love for you. You are the air I breathe. You are the blood that pumps life through my veins. You are the feast of love upon which I dine each and every day of my life. You are the liquid that quenches my thirst, and you are the food that nourishes my body.

Love, Wayne

Lynton closed the laptop, the words written by her beloved in the e-mail ringing in her head as she asked herself why she was at Balete Drive when she could be at Mt. Everest with him.

She looked up at Ms. Grumman as she walked into the breakfast room. She did not even say good morning, but rather asked her pointedly, "You have an idea why Ms. James left?"

.

"No, I know nothing. I wanted not to know; I was glad enough I didn't; and I thanked heaven she was well out of this infernal house and away from that infernal man."

"Yet, you had, then, your idea of her real reason for leaving?"

"Oh, yes as to that. She couldn't have stayed. Fancy it here for a governess! And afterward I imagined and I still imagine. And what I imagine is dreadful."

"Then she left strictly because of him?"

"Yes, he was always hanging on her, doing things in front of the children, unspeakable things. He had no shame. And he also flaunted other women before her. So brazen was he. She was defeated emotionally and psychologically. She simply could endure it no longer and one day she was gone without a word."

What she said made Lynton realize the true depravity of Quincy, but was Ms. James not as depraved? Was she not now back at the house? Had she not risen from hell to return to be by his side?"

It seemed that Lynton was stymied by the monumental task that lay before her. She thought over the matter and put before herself the depths and possibilities of a resolution but there were none at present. She had to keep her head if she should keep nothing else, difficult indeed as it might be in the face of what, in her prodigious experience, was least to be questioned. Late that night, while everyone slept, Lynton had another talk in her room with Ms. Grumman. She began to wonder if Ms. Grumman actually believed she had seen those two entities. After all, Lynton was the only one besides the children to do so.

"Miss, I do not want to doubt you, but there have been rumours about this place for many years, and our minds do play little tricks on us from time to time. Also, you have been under great strain. Could not perhaps all these things have created some imaginary sightings of something that is just in your mind?"

"Did I not give you precise descriptions of the two?"

"You did."

"Are there any pictures in the house of the two?"

"No."

"Then how could I have known what the two looked like? I disclosed minute details."

"You did ma'am. You did."

"And you think I would be able to do that had I not truly seen them?"

LYNTON AND THE GHOSTS
AT THE MANSION ON BALETE DRIVE

Ms. Grumman was so discombobulated they she shook her head in frustration and sighed deeply. She said, "I am sorry miss. I just have heard rumours for years from neighbours about strange things happening around here. I just thought maybe you had heard the same and let your imagination run wild."

"Ms. Grumman, I have kept a secret from you."

"What secret ma'am?"

"I am not whom I appear to be, Ms. Grumman? You see, I came here not just as a governess, but as a searcher of the truth. I am a governess indeed as I have accepted that role, but I am also something else."

"Something else, miss? What do you mean?"

Smiling, Lynton revealed the truth. "Have you heard of Lynton Viñas?"

"My yes, miss – the demon fighter."

"I am she."

"No!"

Nodding her head affirmatively, Lynton said, "Yes."

LYNTON AND THE GHOSTS
AT THE MANSION ON BALETE DRIVE

"Oh my, you have been involved in things like this before. Yes, many times. I have read of your exploits. You are the dynamic dynamo."

"I have encountered much over the years, but never have I been as haunted by any entity from the beyond as I am by these manifestations of evil – pure evil."

In awe of her, Ms. Grumman sat attentively as Lynton encountered her on the ground of a probability that with recurrence, for recurrence was taken for granted, she should get used to her danger, distinctly professing that her personal exposure had suddenly become the least of her discomforts. It was her new suspicion that was intolerable; and yet even to this complication the later hours of the day had brought a little ease. Upon leaving the dumbfounded and awe-struck Ms. Grumman after the discussion and getting her solemn promise not to reveal her true identity, she had of course returned to her pupils, associating the right remedy for her dismay with that sense of their charm which she had already found to be a thing she could positively cultivate and which had never failed her yet. She had simply, in other words, plunged afresh into Flo's special world and put her hand upon the little girl's shoulder in a reassuring way conscious hand straight upon the spot that ached. She had looked up at Lynton in sweet speculation and then a pall swelled onto the

the face somehow, for the first time, showing an indolent look that appeared with a tinge of disdain toward Lynton. Yes, for the first time Lynton felt some mal-intent from her little charge.

She began to gaze into the depths the child's eyes and pronounce their loveliness a trick of premature cunning. Lynton was now becoming guilty of a cynicism in preference to which she naturally preferred to abjure her judgment and, so far as might be, her growing agitation. She found herself, over and over, in the small hours, that with the children's voices in the air, their pressure on one's heart, and their fragrant faces against one's cheek, everything fell to the ground but their incapacity and their beauty. It was a pity that, somehow, to settle this once and for all, she had equally to re-enumerate the signs of subtlety that, in the afternoon, by the pond had made a miracle of her show of self-possession. It was a pity to be obliged to reinvestigate the certitude of the moment itself and repeat how it had come to her as a revelation that the inconceivable communion she witnessed was a matter, for either party, of habit. Yes, Flo and the entity had communicated in their silent way. It was a pity that Lynton should have had to quaver out again the reasons for her not having, in her delusional manner, so much as questioned that the little girl saw their visitant. Flo had intentionally just made Lynton suppose she didn't see the thing across the pond

LYNTON AND THE GHOSTS
AT THE MANSION ON BALETE DRIVE

and at the same time, without showing anything, had Flo even guessed that Lynton had seen the entity? Did she perhaps think Lynton was not privy to the apparition? No, she knew Lynton saw, because the child used portentous little activity to divert Lynton's attention. The perceptible increase of movement, leaving the gazebo, the greater intensity of play were merely diversions instituted by a clever child who wanted to conceal the truth of what was occurring.

Lynton is an astute observer of the sublime, but perhaps this time she was too overcome with concern for her young charges to genuinely see beneath the surface of these two children whom she had grown to love in such a short time. On the other hand, if she had not indulged that intense love, she may have missed the two or three dim elements of comfort that still remained within the children. There was a growing malevolence in them though. Of that she not only deeply sensed, but she could see it in the physical makeup of the two. Yes, their sweet demeanour was still there, but now she sensed that beneath the surface there was something sinister that had taken hold of them.

There was still much she did not know about those two entities as she felt that Ms. Grumman simply was always skirting the real truth. She had only hinted at things, not being overly demonstrative to invoke such further aid to intelligence that might have assisted Lynton even more. She had told her, bit by bit, under pressure, a great deal; but a small shifty spot on the wrong side of it all still sometimes brushed her brow like the wing of a bat.

The sleeping house and the concentration alike of the danger and the shared watchfulness seemed to help. Still, it was like the curtain had only been partially opened. Lynton was determined to pull it open farther. They were at the dining room table sipping pineapple juice when Lynton said, "The situation we are in is very dangerous I am afraid. You know, there's a thing I should require now, just without sparing with you the least bit more and must be frank and get some details that might help me defend the children from this evil. What was it you had in mind when, in our distress, before Milton came back, over the letter from his school, you said, under my insistence, that you didn't pretend for him that he had not literally ever been bad? He has not literally ever, in this short time I have lived here and so closely watched him; been nothing more than an imperturbable little prodigy of delightful, lovable goodness. However, I know there is something within you, something you are holding back. Do not think I shall look upon you as a gossip, someone sharing unproven information. Share with me dear Ms. Grumman. It is vital I know all."

LYNTON AND THE GHOSTS
AT THE MANSION ON BALETE DRIVE

It was a dreadfully austere inquiry, and before the dark led to dawn and admonished us to separate she had her answer. What Ms. Grumman had had in mind proved to be immensely to the purpose. It was neither more nor less than the circumstance that for a period of several months Quincy and the boy had been perpetually together. It was in fact the very appropriate truth that she had ventured to criticize the propriety, to hint at the incongruity, of so close an alliance, and even to go so far on the subject as a frank overture to Miss James about the strangeness of the two seeming to never be apart. The boy even began to share Quincy's room as she would find his bed empty at night only to hear the two talking in low whispers in Quincy's room. Ms. James had, with a most strange manner, requested her to mind her own business. It was then that Ms. Grumman approached Milton directly.

Lynton, titillated with desire for knowledge, said, "And go on then. What happened when you approached Milton?"

"I told him that Quincy was not a good man, and that he should avoid his influence."

"Ah, and I am sure you wistfully reminded him Quincy was a man of many vices and that he should do well to stear clear of him or he be corrupted."

LYNTON AND THE GHOSTS
AT THE MANSION ON BALETE DRIVE

"I did ma'am, but his answer. His answer was so uncharacteristic, so unlike Milton."

"And what were his words?"

Bowing her head and whispering the words, she seemed ashamed. "He just said, 'bitch, mind your own business.' Oh miss, I was so shocked to hear that come from the mouth of him who had never uttered a foul word before as far as I know."

"Did he inform Quincy of your talk?"

"No, not that at all. I was sure, at any rate," she added, "that he didn't. But he denied certain things. He was very strong in his denial. He denied being in Quincy's room and I knew the truth, because I kept a keen eye out every single night. You see, Quincy became his constant companion, only parting from him when he would go out for his debauchery and drinking. It was during Quincy's drunken sprees that I would spend time with Milton, and now little Flo was always with Ms. James. They became inseparable." She sighed and continued. "I kept asking him if he had told Quincy about my concerns, and he kept insisting that he hadn't, but that I needed to remember my station here. He said that if I wasn't extremely careful with my mouth he could get me fired, because his uncle would listen to him."

LYNTON AND THE GHOSTS
AT THE MANSION ON BALETE DRIVE

Lynton reached over and touched Ms. Grumman on the shoulder and said, "I understand your worries."

"Yes ma'am. This is all I have. You know how, in this country, we poor must be eternally vigilant because the rich own our homes, our workplaces and our government. I would be on the streets without this job."

"I can understand, yes. This country and all others make the people bow at the throne of the capitalists. You are a victim as much as poor Flo and Milton. All born without privilege are victims in a world where greed is considered an enviable trait, but there is more to consider here, much more, because I must know everything if I am to battle these demons that have designs on the children."

"Yes ma'am. I understand now that I know who you are. You are here to save the children, and I am willing to do all I can."

"Do you think Milton then either prevaricated about it or out-right lied because he was under the spell of that evil man?"

Her assent was clear enough to cause Lynton's blood to boil as Ms. Grumman said, "He lied, of course"

LYNTON AND THE GHOSTS
AT THE MANSION ON BALETE DRIVE

"And Ms. James?"

"Miss, she simply was so enthralled with Quincy herself that she would do anything he asked. The man was like a hypnotist with her. He would treat her horribly and she'd just come back for more, seeming to almost beg for his ill treatment."

"And did Milton seem equal under Miss James' spell?"

"Oh, he seemed to curry favour with her, but no, he was not mesmerized by her like he was Quincy. But Flo, on the other hand, seemed to be under her spell and less influenced by Quincy."

Now that she had finally opened up, Lynton was firing questions at her like a machine gun spitting bullets of indignation. "So you could see Milton knew what was between the two wretches who seemed to be engaging in debauchery."

"I am not sure ma'am."

"You do know, you dear thing," Lynton replied; "only you haven't my dreadful boldness of mind, and you keep back, out of timidity and modesty and delicacy, even the impression that, in the past, when you had, without my aid, to flounder about in silence, most of all made you miserable. But I shall get it out of you yet! There was something in

J. Wayne Frye

the boy that suggested to you," she continued, "that he covered and concealed their relationship."

"Oh, he couldn't prevent –"

"You from learning the truth? What it shows is that they must, to an almost complete extent, have made him bow to their wishes."

"Ah, Lynton not nice now! I do not want to even entertain the evil goings on in those two's minds. They were so wicked." Ms. Grumman lugubriously pleaded.

"Now I understand when you knew I had that letter from the school why you seemed so timid, so shameful acting. You knew of Milton's evil, evil planted there by that abomination I saw on the balcony and by the window."

"But miss, if he was so bad then as that comes to, how is he such an angel now?"

"Good question, if he was a fiend at school, why? He was free of Quincy's influence there as ghosts are bound to a place, bound to roam and seek solace in familiar surroundings." She lowered her head and sighed before continuing unabated, "How, how, how," Lynton said in her torment, "I am not able to tell you for awhile. Only, put it to me again in the future and I shall hopefully have an answer," she cried in a way that puzzled Ms. Grumman.

"There are directions in which I must not for the present let myself go dear Ms. Grumman. And what of Milton, did he forgive you for your prying and seem to show you respect again?"

"Minimally ma'am, yes. He did not dwell on it nor did I."

"You forgive him because of his youth and the influence exercised by Quincy?"

"I did."

"Ms. Grumman, we must always keep in mind that Milton and Flo are young and impressionable. That is when minds are easily manipulated. The church gets young minds and plants the seeds of fear in them to make sure they are dutiful and follow the dictates of those who tell them how to live their lives. Whom they should hate. Whom they should judge. Whom they should fear. It is an age old ritual practiced by governments among the young, middle-aged and old who must be made complacent in their own slavery. Look at the USA, where fear and propaganda keep people waving the flag and believing it is an exceptional country. Torture, the killing of incidents is all justified and people accept it."

LYNTON AND THE GHOSTS
AT THE MANSION ON BALETE DRIVE

Lynton observed Ms. Grumman's puzzled look and knew her oration of fury at capitalism's evils was simply not understandable to such a simple-minded woman whose meagre means was what kept her and so many like her in complacent slavery to the church, the government and the privileged who controlled her existence. She herself had been unable to see them until her eyes were opened by her beloved Wayne who had spent his life battling against the forces of oppression that kept people so bewildered and defeated that they lined up for their own shackles and chains. She was reared in poverty and ignorance, but she had refused to let it imprison her mind as well as her body. She never accepted the idea that the poor would get their reward in the hereafter. She was more concerned with the here and now. How do you put food on your table? How do you buy milk for your crying baby? How do you put a roof over your head? How to you provide an education and health care for the children the church insists be born but abandons after birth? All that was beyond the understanding of people like Ms. Grumman who sought simple answers for the complex world that kept them in bondage.

Smiling at the bewildered Ms. Grumman, Lynton said, "At all events, almost all the time while Quincy was with Milton, I assume that Flo was always with Ms. James. Am I right in that assumption?"

J. Wayne Frye   105

LYNTON AND THE GHOSTS
AT THE MANSION ON BALETE DRIVE

"Yes, that suited Quincy. He was always obliged by them all."

Lynton's ire was up as the particularly deadly view she was forming made her emotions boil. She was actually trying to forbid herself the entertaining of such evil thoughts, but it was all there. There was no denying it. Shaking her head, she said, "Milton having lied and been impudent are, I confess, less engaging specimens than I had hoped to have from you of the outbreak in him of the evil that took hold. Still," she mused, "They must do, for they make me feel more than ever that I must watch carefully, because though I am a questioner of the church, I am not a questioner of evil. Evil I have confronted since childhood where I suffered the evil of poverty that drove me into the streets to try and get food for my hungry siblings and parents who could not manage to feed the children they elected to have rather than use common sense and birth control. I have never turned from evil. I have always confronted it, and I shall confront it here."

One could see the compassion swelling in Ms. Grumman's teary deep set dark eyes that were blinking incessantly. "Surely miss, you do not think little Milton is truly evil?"

It made Lynton blush to see in her new friend's face how much more unreservedly she had forgiven him than her anecdote struck her as presenting to her own tenderness an occasion for doing. "Evil in actions, rarely, but he is on fire in his mind. He has been carrying on a liaison with evil behind everyone's back."

There was no denying what Lynton saw slowly taking over little Milton's mind. Yes, Quincy was so evil that he came back from the grave to finish corrupting the soul he had set his designs upon. She looked deep into Ms. Grumman's eyes and said, "I fear more for Milton, but I am now also fearful for dear Flo, for what you have said indicates that Ms. James was almost as evil as Quincy."

"Oh no Miss, but she fell under his spell completely."

Lynton was ready to ask the question that had been skirted for so long by Ms. Grumman. "What did she die of? Please, I need to know."

She lowered her head, sighed and almost in a whisper, said, "She killed herself miss. Apparently, she could not endure life without Quincy. She did it in such a horrible way, too."

"Horrible way?"

"Yes, she stood in front of a freight train."

LYNTON AND THE GHOSTS
AT THE MANSION ON BALETE DRIVE

Lynton, always perceptive beyond the norm, said, "And she was naked when she did it, and she left a note saying she was going to join Quincy."

"How did you know ma'am?"

"It is the norm for those whose life becomes a mosaic of debauchery as the lust for the sordid overwhelms them. Also, when they commit suicide, they usually do it in a highly dramatic way. I would say standing naked in front of an on-coming train is highly dramatic. When I saw her across the pond, it was as if she was proud of being evil. There was a darkness within that you could see she delighted in. If you were a religious person, you would start praying at her sight out of fear that the devil was dancing in her mind, ready to devour you. As does Quincy, she delights in evil."

Ms. Grumman took a deep breath and said, "We have a great task ahead of us to protect the little ones don't we? Oh, how are we to defeat this evil?"

"Ms. Grumman, more often than not it is the evil that wins. Yet, at times it comes out second best. We must battle the darkness for the souls of those two little ones."

J. Wayne Frye

LYNTON AND THE GHOSTS
AT THE MANSION ON BALETE DRIVE

CHAPTER 7
THE PRESENCE ON THE LAWN

Lynton's consternation grew with each passing hour. In constant sight of her pupils, without a fresh incident, sufficed to give to grievous fancies and even to odious memories surrendering to their extraordinary childish grace as a thing she could actively cultivate. She made a bold effort to struggle against what she saw as the inevitable coming storm. She wondered how her little charges could help guessing that she thought strange things about them; and the circumstances that these things only made them more interesting was not by itself a direct aid to keeping them in the dark.

Putting things at the worst, at all events, as in meditation she often reminded herself that they were blameless and foredoomed which made her determined to take risks on their behalf. There were moments when, by an irresistible impulse, she found herself catching them up and pressing them to her heart. She could see that they were discombobulated by her often sudden desire to hug them, hold them close. Still, she could sense that within they were harbouring the evil that was trying to consume them. Still, they never once gave any outward manifestation that they were the least bit perturbed or that anything sinister was threatening them.

LYNTON AND THE GHOSTS
AT THE MANSION ON BALETE DRIVE

The hours of peace that she still enjoyed was heartening as the immediate charm of her companions was a beguilement still effective even under the shadow of the possibility that it was all fake. They were, at this period, extravagantly and preternaturally fond of her. They wanted to do so many things for their protectress; though they got their lessons better and better, which was naturally what would please her most, in the way of diverting, entertaining, surprising her; reading her passages, telling her stories, playing games, and above all, astonishing her by the pieces they had secretly got by heart and could interminably recite. Still, there was always something sinister beneath the surface, as if Lynton expected a cataclysmic explosion of emotion and turmoil at any minute.

It almost began to appear that the evil had somehow been abated as the children seemed so happy. And Lynton was happy too. Most of all, she delighted in Milton's exuberance and his perpetually striking show of cleverness.

For a long time she had wondered about the "why" of his being kicked out of school, but she was fearful of bringing it up and spoiling the now sanguine merriment they all shared, as the young often do heartless things without mal-intent. She saw no need to cause him embarrassment and consternation. Still, it preyed upon her mind. It danced in her head like a waltz of doubt.

J. Wayne Frye

LYNTON AND THE GHOSTS
AT THE MANSION ON BALETE DRIVE

For days they lived in a cloud of music, love, success and private theatricals. The musical sense in each of the children was of the quickest, but the elder, in particular, had a marvellous knack of plucking the guitar, and with the piano he broke into delightful fancies.

They were both extraordinary, and they never quarrelled or complained. Still, there was something deceptive going on. Lynton observed that there were traces of little understandings between them by which one of them should keep her occupied while the other slipped away. However, all this was the quiet before a storm. Now, in going on with the record of what was hideous on Balete Drive, there seemed to come a time when all joy morphed into suffering.

One evening, with nothing to lead up or to prepare for it, Lynton felt the cold touch of the impression that had breathed on her the night she saw Quincy walking across the balcony. In a huge alcove, just off from the study, there was a room full of old books. She was surprised to see Wayne Frye's very first book on the shelf and she took it down, reclined in an overstuffed chair and began to read. It was very late and though she was deeply interested in the author, she found herself, at the turn of a page deciding to go to her room. She meandered up the stairs to her room to continue to read in the flickering light that came from a few lights left on to guide people in the darkness up the stairs. She strolled into her room and sat down in the chair by the window, continuing to read. Looking up suddenly from the book and scanning the room, she listened, reminded of the faint sense she had the first night, of there being something indefinably astir in the house, and noted the soft breath of air was causing the curtain on the window to flutter. Then, with all the marks of a deliberation that must have seemed magnificent had there been anyone to admire it, she laid down her book, rose to her feet, and, taking the small flashlight on the nightstand, went straight out of the room and noiselessly closed the door.

It cannot be determined what guided her, but she went straight along the hallway, not turning on lights but rather holding the flashlight high, until she came within sight of the tall window that presided over the great turn of the staircase. At this point she precipitately found herself aware of some things. They were practically simultaneous, yet they had flashes of succession. Her flashlight, under a bold flourish, went out, and she perceived, by the uncovered window, that the yielding dusk of earliest morning rendered it unnecessary. Without it, the next instant, she saw that there was someone on the stairs. She stiffened herself, for she knew she was about to have her third encounter with Quincy. The apparition had reached the landing halfway up and was therefore on the spot nearest the window, where at sight of her, it stopped short and fixed upon her exactly as it had fixed upon her from the balcony and through the window. He knew her as well as she knew him; and so, in the cold, faint twilight, with a glimmer in the high glass and another on the polish of the oak stair below, they faced each other in common intensity. He was absolutely, on this occasion, a deplorable, detestable, dangerous presence. The evil was all about him as if he was cloaked in it.

She had plenty of anguish after that extraordinary moment, but she had no terror. After all, this was the dynamic dynamo. She felt, in a fierce rigor of confidence, that if she stood her ground he would know she was not going to yield to his evil. The dead silence of their long gaze at such close quarters gave into the horror of it all though. Entity against demon fighter, this was a test of wills. If she had met a murderer in such a place and at such an hour, they still at least would have spoken. Something would have passed between them; if nothing had passed, one of them would have moved. The moment was so prolonged that it would have taken but little more to make her think she was dreaming. The silence itself, which was indeed in a manner an attestation of her strength as she refused to scream in horror, no doubt confused Quincy.

LYNTON AND THE GHOSTS
AT THE MANSION ON BALETE DRIVE

The test of wills made the apparition turn as if it had been in receipt of an order not to pass. With villainous eyes looking back as it turned, there was a hatred that cut through to the bone. The abomination descended straight down the staircase and into the darkness below.

Lynton remained awhile at the top of the stairs, but with the effect presently of understanding that her visitor had gone. Then she prepared to return to her room. Instinctively, on the way, she stopped by Flo's room, slowly opened the door and peeped in. Flo's little bed was empty; and on this sight she caught her breath. She perceived an agitation of the window curtains that hung to the floor of the window on the far wall, and the child, ducking down, emerged rosily from the other side of it. Flo stood there, looking intensely grave, and Lynton had a sense of lost advantage. Then, Flo, in a scolding manner said, "My naughty, naughty ma'am, where have you been?"

"Never mind me. Why were you out of bed?"

"I was scared. I went to your room and you were not there."

"No I wasn't. I was tending to a serious matter."

"Oh miss," she said with earnestness, "no matter is so serious you should be up in the darkness."

J. Wayne Frye

LYNTON AND THE GHOSTS
AT THE MANSION ON BALETE DRIVE

She tucked Flo back in bed, and went to her room. She dropped back into her chair, feeling a little faint; and then Flo was standing at the door. She pattered straight over to Lynton, threw herself upon her knee, and softly lay her head on Lynton's left breast.

Lynton closed her eyes an instant, yieldingly, consciously to her thoughts. She slowly opened them and said, "You were at the window looking out weren't you?"

"Yes."

"Why were you looking out? What were you looking for?"

"I don't know. I just felt someone was out there."

Looking directly in her eyes, Lynton said, "And did you see anyone?"

"Ah, no," she returned, almost with the full privilege of childish inconsequence, with resentfulness hanging on her words, though with tinge of sweetness in her little drawl of the negative. At that moment, in the state of her nervousness, Lynton absolutely believed she lied; and she mulled over the three or four possible ways in which she might take this up. One of these, for a moment, tempted her with such singular intensity that, to withstand it, she gripped Flo with a hug of doubt, wonderfully, she submitted to it without a cry or a sign of fright. She thought to herself, why not break out at her on the spot and have it all over? Yes, give it to her straight in her lovely little lighted face that she knew she was looking for Ms. James. Yet, as she was about to utter those words, the solicitation dropped, alas, as quickly as it came. Had she succumbed to the notion and carried it through she might have spared herself some future heartache.

Instead of succumbing to the urge, she sprang again to her feet, and carried Flo over to her bed, looked at her bed, and took a helpless middle way. She asked as she gently laid her on the bed, "Why did you pull the curtain over yourself, hiding behind it. Why not just open it to look out?"

Flo luminously considered; after which, with her little divine smile, she said, "Because, because, well, I don't know."

"Who were you really looking for?"

Flo looked up at her and Lynton could tell before the words were even uttered that they were a lie. "Well, I just figured you were out walking around the grounds. I just wanted to see what you were doing. That's all."

LYNTON AND THE GHOSTS
AT THE MANSION ON BALETE DRIVE

The lie was compounded when Flo continued. "Oh, I just wanted to know where you were my dear. That is all." Her eyes sparkled with the depth of her lie as she continued. "Why you are such a dear to me. I am concerned about you. Just a few days ago at the pond, I could see you were worried about something. I think you worry too much."

And after a little while, when Flo had pulled the covers up, Lynton reached down to take her little hand. It was as cold as ice. Oh, the evil, thought Lynton, was taking hold of her.

Flo drifted off to sleep, and Lynton went back to sit in the chair, but only intermittently, as at selected moments when her roommate unmistakably was sleeping, she would steal out, take noiseless turns in the hallway and stand gazing at the spot where she had seen Quincy. She would never meet him there again; and on no other occasion would she see him in the house. She just greeted, on the staircase, on the other hand, a different adventure. Looking down from the top of the stairs she at once recognized the presence of a woman seated on one of the lower steps with her back presented to her, her body half-bowed and her head, in an attitude of woe, in her hands. The woman was there but an instant, however, she vanished without looking round at her. She knew, nonetheless, exactly what dreadful person it was.

LYNTON AND THE GHOSTS
AT THE MANSION ON BALETE DRIVE

She wondered whether, if instead of standing and looking silently that perhaps she could have called out Ms. James, for it was she who was there. But why was she there? Yes, she had come inside to look for Flo and was remorseful she had not found her.

. On the very next night after her latest encounter with that gentleman and woman she faced one of her most alarming incidents that perilously proved quite her sharpest shock. She was weary with watching for any signs of the entities. She lay in a deep sleep until she heard the old grandfather clock chime one in the morning and she arose from her slumber. She had left a light burning, but it was now out, and she felt an instant certainty that Flo, who had slept with her again, had turned it off. This brought her to her feet and she looked over to see Flo was gone. A glance at the window enlightened her further, as the child had again gotten up, and was again squeezed in behind the curtains and was peering out into the night. She now was looking so intensely out the window that she was not even disturbed when Lynton turned on the light. Hidden, protected, absorbed, Flo rested on the sill as the casement opened forward and gave herself up. There was a great still moon to help her, and this fact had counted in Lynton's quick decision. Flo was face to face with the apparition from the lake, and could now communicate with it as she had not then been able

J. Wayne Frye

to do. What Lynton, on her side, had to care for was, without disturbing her, to reach, from the corridor, some other window in the same direction.

She got to the door without disturbing Flo. As Lynton stood in the hallway, she had her eyes on Milton's door, which was but ten steps off and which, indescribably, produced the strange impulse to march into his room. She wondered if his bed was also empty and he too was secretly at watch, looking out his window. It was a deep, soundless minute, at the end of which her impulse failed. He was quiet; he might be innocent; the risk was hideous; she turned away. There was a something on the grounds and Lynton needed to deal with it. There were empty rooms, and it was only a question of choosing the right one. The right one suddenly presented itself to her as the lower one, which was high above the gardens and looked out toward the pond. This was a large, square chamber, arranged with some state as a bedroom, the extravagant size of which made it so inconvenient that it had not for years, though kept by Ms. Grumman in exemplary order, been occupied. She had often admired it and she knew her way about in it. She unbolted the door as quietly as she could, walked over and opened the shutter blinds on the large window. She applied her face to the window pane, to see she had a grand view of the whole garden and pond in the distance. Then she saw it. The moon made the night extraordinarily penetrable and showed her on the lawn a person, diminished by distance, who stood there motionless and as if fascinated, looking up to where she appeared, looking, that is, not so much straight at her as at something that was apparently above her. There was clearly another person above her on the third floor balcony attracting the attention of the individual in the garden, but the presence on the lawn was not in the least what she had conceived and had confidently hurried to meet. The presence on the lawn was no other than little Milton himself.

J. Wayne Frye

CHAPTER 8
SPHERE OF EVIL

Lynton was in shock. She stood in awe, knowing who was on the balcony above hypnotically mesmerizing Milton. She asked herself whether she should call out to Milton, and she elected to wait for awhile just to see how far things were going to go. She did not have to wait long. Milton lowered his head, turned and headed back toward the house, almost marching with military precision. He stopped for a second and obviously looked up at Flo who, no doubt, was still looking out the window. Lynton left the room, stood in the hall for awhile until she heard the front door open, then she made her way back to her bedroom, and was surprised to see Flo curled up in bed, appearing to be fast asleep, which was obviously an act. She stood by her door and heard Milton walk down the hall, then gently close his bedroom door.

Lynton walked over to the chair, took a seat, eased back, sighed and slowly drifted off to sleep. She spent a restless night pondering what all this meant. About dawn, she got up and walked to the window, looked out in the garden and there she saw Ms. James in very faint outline way across the other side of the pond. She was looking toward the house longingly. The fog covered her and she slowly faded from view.

LYNTON AND THE GHOSTS
AT THE MANSION ON BALETE DRIVE

She spoke to Mrs. Grumman. The rigor with which she kept her pupils in sight made it often difficult to talk to her privately of what happened during the night. Ms. Grumman was shocked by what she heard, and even asked if maybe Lynton had not been dreaming. Empathically indicating there was no chance of that, Ms. Grumman reached out and took her hand as she surveyed the children with an intense stare, her large brown arms folded and a concerned look on her face.

Flights of fancy occupied the children as both adults whispered that it would be best at present not to bring up what had occurred the previous night. The two women went onto the terrace where, with the lapse of the season, the afternoon sun was now agreeable; and they sat there together while, before them, at a distance, but within call if they wished, the children strolled to and fro in one of their most manageable moods. They moved slowly, in unison, below them, over the lawn, the boy, as they went, reading aloud from a storybook and passing his arm round his sister to keep her quite. Mrs. Grumman watched them with positive placidity; then she caught the suppressed intellectual creak with which she conscientiously turned to take from Lynton a view of the book she was reading by her beloved Wayne. To Lynton, the two of them were equal in every way, but Ms. Grumman had long ago been taught to bow before those with more authority so there was an odd

J. Wayne Frye

recognition of Lynton's superior position in the rank of the social ladder. It was always difficult for those who were relegated to a lower socio-economic status to not think somehow they were not worthy, but Lynton always said she never saw any one who was beneath her, and likewise, she never saw anyone who was above her. She lived a truly equalitarian existence. You could tell that Ms. Grumman was growing in respect for this extraordinary woman who captivated and enthralled all who came within her sphere.

In fact, Ms. Grumman was becoming so relaxed around Lynton that she offered her mind to her disclosures as if she wished to mix a witch's broth and proposed it with assurance in a saucepan of respect. This had become thoroughly her attitude by the time that, in Lynton's recital of the events of the night, she reached the point of what Milton had been standing there in the garden looking up at. She suddenly stopped, and she determinedly looked over at Ms. Grumman, "Enough, I am confronting him."

"Are you sure miss.?"

Not answering, she marched over to Milton. Forcefully, she said, "Milton, what were you doing in the garden last night?"

He turned from her, walked away with a shrug

of his shoulders, saying nothing. She walked up beside him as they strolled away from Flo who was skipping along the edge of the pond. Why, she thought, was he ignoring her? Surely he knew that she was aware that the previous night Quincy was hungrily hovering on the balcony silently communicating with him.

Not a sound, as they walked, had passed between them, and she wondered if he was groping about in his little mind for something plausible and not too grotesque to tell her. It would tax his invention, certainly, and she felt, this time, over his real embarrassment, a curious thrill of triumph as she exalted in causing him some consternation as it was good that he was struggling with the truth now. It was a sharp trap for the inscrutable. He couldn't play any longer at innocence; so how would he get out of it? There beat in Lynton indeed, with the passionate throb of this question an equal appeal of how she would handle what he said. She stopped, put her hands on his shoulders and turned him toward her. He thought he could do what he liked, with all his cleverness to help him. Yet, Lynton was now ready to confront him directly. "You must tell me now and it must be the truth. What did you go out for last night? What were you doing out in the garden."

"My, you sound cross with me."

LYNTON AND THE GHOSTS
AT THE MANSION ON BALETE DRIVE

"No, I am not cross, only curious."

He let out a beautiful smile, his eyes began to twinkle, and the uncovering of his little teeth shined in the fading daylight. "If I tell you why, will you understand?"

Lynton's heart, at this, leaped into her mouth. Would he really tell her why? She found no sound on her lips to press it, and she replied only with a vague, repeated, grimacing nod. He was gentleness itself, and while she wagged her head at him he stood there more than ever seemingly someone far beyond his meagre years. It was his brightness indeed that gave her respite. Was he really going to tell her the truth?

"Well," he said at last, "just exactly in what order should I do this."

"Do what?"

"You think of me as bad." There was a sweetness and gaiety with which he brought out the word, as he leaped up and kissed her on the cheek. It was practically the end of everything. She met his kiss and she had to make, while she folded him for a minute in her arms, the most stupendous effort not to cry. He had given exactly the account of himself that permitted least of her going behind it, and it was then that she knew she had to say it. "Why Milton would you go out in the dark like that? It is dangerous."

"My oh my, don't you know we were playing a game with you? That is all, just a game. I told Flo to get up and go to the window and I'd be looking up. We thought it would be frightful fun to get you all confused."

"And when did you go down?"

"At midnight just as we planned."

"I see, but how could you be sure I would know you two were up?"

"Oh, I arranged that with Flo." His answers rang out with an assuredness that actually made Lynton marvel at his ability to bend the truth. "She was to get up and look out."

"Which is what she did," said Lynton grudgingly admiring his ability to hide the truth.

"So she disturbed you, and, to see what she was looking at, you also looked and you saw me."

"While you," she concurred, "were both laughing at my expense?"

"I am afraid we were dear."

LYNTON AND THE GHOSTS
AT THE MANSION ON BALETE DRIVE

He literally bloomed with pride over the exploit that he seemed intent on lying about. Oh, he was good thought Lynton. So good that she could not help but admire his wiliness and uncanny ability at manipulative lying.

Smiling broadly, he said, "It was a grand and glorious trick was it not?"

"Not," said Lynton as she turned and told him they needed to go inside.

Milton, smiling, took her hand and said, "Don't be cross dear lady. After all, we are just silly little children who had fun at your expense. Obviously we should be punished I suppose."

Then, he did something very sinister. In an almost whisper, like he was trying to conceal it, he said, "There is no telling what I might do, you know. I gave them a taste of that at school awhile ago. I did."

He was so good, so very good. Lynton looked over at Flo who was observing the two of them closely. She had a quizzical look on her face, and Lynton wondered if she asked Flo the same questions if her story would coincide with Milton's. They were both wily and Lynton was slowly learning that the façade of nice, dainty, mannerly, dutiful little children was a result of being exposed to two wicked people – Quincy and Ms. James.

It was obvious to Milton she was displeased, but she took his hand and then she bent down to embrace him. He responded to it by pulling her in a seemingly adult manner closer to him, almost as if he wanted her to know he was not just a little boy. She was bothered by it. Was it the evil influence of that abomination that had been on the balcony above that night? Oh, how she wanted to reach out and shake him, call him a bold-faced liar, but that would only drive him further into the sphere of evil that had descend upon the house on Balete Drive.

CHAPTER 9
PIT OF DARKNESS

The particular impression Lynton had from her conversation with Milton was conveyed in the morning light to Ms. Grumman. "Everything lies in half a dozen words he uttered," she said to her, "words that really settle the matter."

"What words, ma'am?"

"He said, 'There is no telling what I might do, you know. I gave them a taste of that at school awhile ago.' It was devilish the way he said it. "

Ms. Grumman, put her right hand to her mouth as she uttered, "Oh my."

"The four of them, yes, the four of them are plotting, but plotting what?"

"What could they be plotting?"

"I believe they are plotting to turn their souls over to those two evil entities. For some reason, those entities want those children in the worst sort of way."

Ms. Grumman was overwhelmed now with despair. "You are a demon fighter. Surely you know how to fight this evil?"

LYNTON AND THE GHOSTS
AT THE MANSION ON BALETE DRIVE

"All I know is that the four of them are conspiring, but conspiring to do what, where and when? The four meet and without speech they plan and plot If on either of these last nights you had been with either child, you would clearly have understood. The more I've watched and waited the more I've felt that if there were nothing else to make it sure it would be made so by the systematic silence of each about what is happening. Never, by a slip of the tongue, have they so much as alluded to either of their old friends, any more than Milton has alluded to his expulsion from school for the commitment of ill deeds. Oh, yes, we may sit here and look at them, and they may show off to us to their fill; but even while they are pretending to be lost in their fairytales they're steeped in their vision of the dead restored. When they are whispering, they are whispering of horrors! I go on, I know, as if I were crazy; and it's a wonder I'm not. What I've seen would have made many people crazy for sure. However, I have become more lucid each day, as the evil becomes clearer and more pronounced."

Lynton felt tenseness in Ms. Grumman. It seemed more than she could comprehend. She said, "Pray tell me all that you have discovered."

"So much has mystified and troubled me. They are more than earthly perfection. It is unnatural in two children. It's a game."

J. Wayne Frye

LYNTON AND THE GHOSTS
AT THE MANSION ON BALETE DRIVE

"Oh miss. They are such little darlings that are so good."

"Oh no, they haven't been good. They've only been playing at good. It has been easy to live with them, because they're simply leading a life of their own. They're not mine. They're not ours. They're his and they're hers!"

"You mean Quincy and Ms. James?"

"Of course!"

"You mean they want them?"

"Yes."

"But for what?"

"For the love of all the evil that, in those dreadful days, the pair put into them and into themselves. And to ply them with that evil still, to keep up the work of demons, is what brings them here. I have faced evil before but never evil as insidious, as unmitigated, as pervasive as that exhibited here by those two abominations that are from the very darkest corners of the pit of damnation."

"Oh miss. I am afraid for them, afraid for us too."

LYNTON AND THE GHOSTS
AT THE MANSION ON BALETE DRIVE

"I am working on it in my mind good woman."

"I knew they were practicing evil. I should have reported it, but I was afraid. I did go to church though and asked for divine intervention."

Shaking her head, Lynton said, "The church is rarely the help it should be I am afraid. Relying on yourself is often a more appropriate approach. It does not matter now. What is done is done. What we must do is move forward from here with all due haste."

"But they were evil and I knew it. Still, they are dead. What can the dead do?"

"Do?" Lynton echoed so loud that Milton and Flo, as they passed at a distance, paused an instant in their walk and looked at them. "Don't they do enough?" She whispered, while the children, having smiled and nodded and kissed hands to them, resumed their play. "They can destroy them!" At this her companion did turn, but the inquiry she launched was a silent one, the effect of which was to make Lynton more explicit. "They don't know, as yet, quite how, but they're trying hard. They're seen only across, as it were, and beyond, in strange places and on high places, the balcony, the outside of windows, the further edge of pools; but there's a deep design, on either side, to shorten the distance and overcome the obstacle;

and the success of the tempters is only a question of time."

"For the children to come?"

"Yes, unless we can intercede."

"We must contact Mr. Delmonte. He must get them out of here."

Ms. Grumman stood still, staring and thinking. "He is a hard man ma'am. To be frank he cares not at all for them. But maybe if you contacted him? You do have his e-mail do you not?"

"I do, and I will. I shall tell him that his house is poisoned and his nephew and niece are for all practical purposes going mad."

"Tell him he should be here as soon as possible so that he can save them. Ah, but I fear his reaction. He can be so heartless."

"He is no good then. He will not help. I can see that. He wanted me here so he could be free of them. Why I think he may well know what is going on. Yes, I believe he may have seen the entities himself and just cast it aside without care or worry. As you say, when it comes to the children he can be heartless and uncaring. No, I shall not contact him. We fight this alone."

LYNTON AND THE GHOSTS
AT THE MANSION ON BALETE DRIVE

Lynton turned decisively, "Yes, I shall not ask his help, because I think he may do more harm than good."

Now, the decision was wilfully made by Lynton. This would be a battle she would wage mostly alone. Often she had her two dear friends, Channa and Ingrid, by her side, but this time they were out of the country, and she would have to rely only on Ms. Grumman for support.

Lynton knew the entities were aware of her predicament and this strange knowledge preyed heavily upon her weary mind. And the children were aware too. They knew, but did not reveal. The element of the unnamed and untouched hung heavily over all of them, and that so much avoidance could not have been so successfully effected without a great deal of tacit arrangement. It was as if, at moments, they were all perpetually coming into sight of subjects before which they must stop short, turning suddenly out of alleys that were perceived to be blind, closing with a little bang that made them look at each other in bewilderment as if they all wanted to reveal the obvious, to scream it out, but they did not. All conversation skirted forbidden ground. Forbidden ground was the question of the return of the dead in general and of whatever, in special, might survive, in memory, of the friends little children had lost. There were days when she could have

J. Wayne Frye

sworn that one of them had, with a small invisible nudge, said to the other: "She thinks she'll reveal herself to us, but she won't."

Lynton had never broached the subject of either entity, and she was waiting for just the right time to do it, to shock them into the reality of what they were acquiescing to.

The children had a delightful endless appetite for passages in Lynton's history, to which she had again and again treated them. They were in possession of everything that had ever happened to her since childhood, with every circumstance the story of her smallest adventures and of those of her brother and sisters, as well as many particulars of the eccentric nature of her having to leave home at 12. There were things enough, taking one with another, to chatter about, if one went very fast and knew by instinct when to go round. They pulled with an art of their own the strings of her invention and her memory; and nothing else perhaps, when she thought of such occasions afterward, gave her the suspicion of being watched from under cover. The entities were not physically present, but they were always hovering somewhere, waiting to pounce on that one moment when all was ripe for conquest of the little souls. It was a tedious and taxing battle that Lynton bore in almost lonely silence. It seemed Ms. Grumman had mostly deserted her.

LYNTON AND THE GHOSTS
AT THE MANSION ON BALETE DRIVE

The days passed for her without another encounter. There had been no manifestation since the light brush, that night on the upper landing, of the presence of a woman at the foot of the stairs. There was many a corner around which she expected to come upon Quincy, and many a situation that, in a merely sinister way, would have favoured the appearance of Ms. James. The spring had turned and was slowly fading away. The place, with its grey sky and withered gardens, its bared spaces and scattered weeds, was like a theatre after the performance, deserted and silent. There were exactly states of the air, conditions of sound and of stillness, unspeakable impressions of something that was about to explode. She recognized the signs, the portents of the coming calamity. Still she remained unaccompanied and empty, and she continued unmolested; if unmolested one could call a young woman whose sensibility had, in the most extraordinary fashion, not declined but deepened. She had said in her talk with Ms. Grumman on that horrid scene of Flo's by the lake and had perplexed her by so saying that it would from that moment distress her. She had then expressed what was vividly in her mind: the truth that, whether the children really saw or not as there was never any outward indication they had ever seen the entities. Yet, Lynton knew they had. Still, there was never any indication other than their whispering and their creeping about in various secluded places.

J. Wayne Frye

LYNTON AND THE GHOSTS
AT THE MANSION ON BALETE DRIVE

Within Lynton was a growing obsession. There were times when they were all together when she would have been ready to swear that, literally, in her presence, but with her direct sense of it closed, they had visitors who were known and were welcome. This occurred just when she happened to be out of their sight. Then, when she came back into their sight, the low, indelicate whispers would stop and there would be a sinister lull of silence, as if all three of them were waiting for an explosion of some sort.

She so often wanted to cry out "They are here, and I know it."

Still, there was a conscious denial on their part, but subconsciously she wondered if they were also in denial. Their denial was so complete in the sociability and their tenderness, in just the crystal depths of which like the flash of a fish in a stream the mockery of their advantage peeped up. The shock, in truth, had sunk into Lynton still deeper than she knew on the night when, looking out to see either Quincy or Ms. James under the stars, she had beheld the boy over whose rest she watched and who had immediately brought in with him the lovely upward look with which, from the balcony above her, the hideous apparition of Quincy had played. If it was a question of a scare, her discovery on that occasion had scared her more than any other, and it was in the condition of nerves produced by it that she made her actual deductions.

She approached it from one side and the other, always mulling over what to do, but what could she do, but see it through as she was waiting for the inevitable. As the names of those two abominations died away on her lips, she said to herself that she should indeed help them to represent something infamous, if, by pronouncing them, she should violate a rare case of instinctive delicacy. No, she could not bring herself to do it. They were only children fighting against evil that was trying to swarm them, embrace them and drag them into the pit of darkness.

CHAPTER 10
SHE KNEW WHAT HE MEANT

There was a serene madness to Lynton's existence now, as she drifted into stillness, a pause of all life so to speak. She also sensed that the others, the outsiders, were there. What it was most impossible to get rid of was the cruel idea that, whatever she had seen, Milton and Flo saw much more, things terrible and not guessable and that sprang from dreadful passages of intercourse in the past when they were completely under those two's power.. Such things naturally left on the surface, for the time, a chill which they vociferously denied feeling; and they had, all three, with repetition, gotten into such splendid training that they went, each time, almost automatically, to mark the close of the incident, through the very same movements. It was striking of the children, at all events, to kiss Lynton inveterately with a kind of wild irrelevance and never to fail. Once though, when he was unguarded, Milton looked at her unexpectedly and said, "Where is he?"

Lynton replied, "Who?"

Shaking his head, Milton said, "Oh, what did I say?"

"You asked where he is."

LYNTON AND THE GHOSTS
AT THE MANSION ON BALETE DRIVE

"Did I? Oh, don't know what I meant."

Extraordinary woman that she was, Lynton never lost patience with the children. Adorable they were; nobody could hate them. The routine of waiting for something to happen was beginning to wear thin on her. But relief arrived, though it was only the relief that a snap brings to a strain or the burst of a thunderstorm to a day of suffocation. It was at least change, and it came with a rush.

Now, Lynton was not one given to attending church, but she felt it might be advisable to take the children to church as a way of seeing just how they would react in an atmosphere that was supposedly counter to the one which had been trapping them for so long in the clutches of evil. Granted, she thought, too often the church perpetrated evil itself in the form of judgmental arrogance and refusal to confront socio-economic disparity, but it was important to see just how the children might react.

Walking to church, she had had Milton at her side and his sister, in advance of them skipping merrily along and Mrs. Grumman slightly behind all of them as she was enjoying the cool morning air. It was a crisp, clear day, the first of its order for some time; the night had actually clung to the day in a way with the coolness and the air, bright and sharp, made the church bells almost gay. It

J. Wayne Frye

was an odd accident thought Lynton that should have happened at such a moment to be particularly and very gratefully struck with the obedience of her little charges.

She had all but pinned the boy to her side. She was like a goalkeeper with an eye to possible surprises on the field of honour where men and women placed all energy in putting a ball into a net that represented victory. Milton was the striker with the ball in his control, but the net, for him, did not represent victory but surrender to the malevolent forces of those two abominations. Not realizing it, Lynton was about to witness the rise if a curtain which would introduce a horrifying play on the stage upon which this drama was about to play out.

The incident was precipitated when Milton said, "Look here, my dear, when in the world, please, am I going back to school?"

What he said probably sounded harmless enough, particularly as uttered in the sweet, high, casual voice, but there was something that made one "catch," and she caught, at any rate, now so effectually that she stopped as short as if one of the trees of the park had fallen across the road. There was something new, on the spot, between them, and he was perfectly aware that she recognized it, though, to enable her to do so, he had no need to look less candid and charming than usual. She could feel in him how he already, from her at first finding nothing to reply, perceived the advantage he had gained. She was so slow to find anything that he had plenty of time, after a minute, to continue with his suggestive but inconclusive smile: "You know, my dear, I should really be back at school. I should."

"You think you should, uh?"

"Yes, I do, because I think you are getting frightfully attached to me. Why, if I did not know better, I would think you were kidnapping me for your own enjoyment, my dear."

"But if you went back to school, wouldn't you miss something that is at your home on Balete Drive?"

Lynton thought that might make him admit to the presence of Quincy. He replied to her dismay, "Well, you and Flo of course would be missed, but I am growing up and need the stimulation of my peers."

Lynton began to bore in. "But is there not someone else whom you would miss? Someone I am not supposed to know about?"

Without hesitations he said, "No one."

LYNTON AND THE GHOSTS
AT THE MANSION ON BALETE DRIVE

Lynton stopped, laid her hand on his shoulder, and said, "I speak of the unspeakable Milton."

"My goodness, you are speaking in riddles today."

"There is no riddle Milton. I speak of that night."

"You mean when I went into the garden, when Flo and I played our little joke on you?"

"That one night?"

"When I went down - went out of the house?"

"Yes."

He got a distant look on his face, and spoke as if in a trance. "It was nothing but a joke – a joke on you my dear, and you fell for it. You know I could do it again. I mean play a joke on you."

"Oh, yes, you could."

A sinister look crept across his face and he seemed to age. He was no longer a little boy, but a man. Even his voice deepened. "I can do it again. I can. You have no idea what I am capable of with his help. Yes, with his help I am capable of the diabolical."

Now she had him. "He? Who is he?"

Instantly he seemed to return to little boy mode. "He? I must have misspoken my dear."

Oh, she had been so close to getting him to admit he was convening with Quincy, but that moment was gone now. They resumed their walk as Milton said, "Then am I going back?"

"Were you happy there, Milton?"

"I'm happy anywhere, my dear."

"Well, then," Lynton offered, "if you're just as happy here, why go back?"

"Ah, but that isn't everything! You know something and I know you do."

"Do I?"

"You are just being coy," Milton said matter-of-factly.

"Coy about what?"

"My dear, come on now. You know what."

"No Milton, maybe I don't have any idea what you are talking about."

LYNTON AND THE GHOSTS
AT THE MANSION ON BALETE DRIVE

Then, he simply changed the focus of the conversation. "I need to go back to experience more life, more excitement."

"I see," Lynton said as they arrived within sight of the church and of various persons. Had the moment of truth been lost? They would have to be silent now, but she felt as they walked down the aisle that a certain door had finally been opened. Then, as they stopped at a pew and entered, he looked up at her and said, "I want to be with others like me."

She whispered as they seated themselves, "There are not many like you Milton. The only one I know who can see the things you do is Flo."

He whispered in reply, "You really compare me to a baby girl?"

Church began and a reply from Lynton never came. All through the service, she, as usual, ignored the rhetoric that was laced with hate for a society that was filled with the sins of the flesh, but made no mention of the sins of omission like poverty, unequal income distribution, corruption and the cow-towing by government to the society of greed that trapped all within its demonic like tentacles that gobble up everything in its sight in the unquenchable pursuit of the privileged class for more and more.

LYNTON AND THE GHOSTS
AT THE MANSION ON BALETE DRIVE

They left the church after the service and strolled through the graveyard with its old, thick graves. While the others strolled on, Lynton and Milton paused, on the path from the gate, by a low, oblong, table-like tomb. Milton was looking with great intent at the tomb. He dropped straight down on the stone slab, as if suddenly to rest. "I know what you think."

Lynton, very calmly replied, "How do you know what I think?"

"Ah, well, of course I don't; for it strikes me you never tell me. But you know what I mean."

"Know what, Milton?"

"Know about unmentionable things. You are a sensitive person. You see and hear things that others don't. You also can feel things others don't. You are kind and caring, but sometimes the kind and caring suffer great blows of agony in their hearts for being too sensitive. Sometimes they imagine things too. Things that are not there in reality appear to them to reinforce their perceptions.

"And you think I may imagine things, Milton?

"Yes, I do indeed. I think you sometimes let your imagination run wild."

J. Wayne Frye

LYNTON AND THE GHOSTS
AT THE MANSION ON BALETE DRIVE

"Oh, you do, uh?

"Yes, you do my dear. I think you imagine all kinds of things – evil things. You sometimes live in a fanciful world, you do." Now, seemingly disinterested with that line of thought, he continued, "Why the way I'm going on. You know, I wonder what my uncle would think about how you are acting toward me and Flo?

"Frankly, I don't think your uncle much cares."

"You know him well. He cares so little about us. We are just an obligation, and he'd be glad to be shut of us."

"You think he is that heartless."

"I do."

Suddenly, Lynton felt such sorrow for the boy. She bent down, pulled him up, wrapped her arms around him and said, "I am sorry Milton. It is not easy being on your own at your age, and you are on your own, because your parents are no more, and your uncle has deserted you, but I will not."

He let go of Lynton, started walking toward the others in the distance, looked back over his shoulder and said, "Oh, I am not alone. No, I am not alone at all."

Oh, she knew what he meant. Yes, he had Quincy and Ms. James.

LYNTON AND THE GHOSTS
AT THE MANSION ON BALETE DRIVE

CHAPTER 11
QUESTION MY VERACITY

The fate of all was practically settled from the moment she never followed him. It was a pitiful surrender to agitation, but her being aware of this had somehow no power to restore her. She only stood there and read into what her little friend had said. She felt herself a failure, because she had not seized upon the opportunity to expose the truth to him, let him know she would not cower in fear if only he would reach out to her and admit what was happening.

She had sat out to get Milton to open up, but in reality, he had only closed the door again with a loud thud of indifference. He had got out of her that there was something she was much afraid of and that he should probably be able to make use of her fear to gain, for his own purpose, more freedom to do as he desired. Her fear was of having to deal with the intolerable question of the grounds of his dismissal from school, for that was really the key question of the horrors gathered behind. The boy, to her deep discomposure, was immensely in the right, was in a position to say to her, "Either you clear up with my guardian the mystery of this interruption of my studies, or you cease to expect me to lead with you a life that's so unnatural for a boy. I shall not permit you to control me or my actions." What was so unnatural

J. Wayne Frye   149

now was Lynton's revelation of a determined plan on Milton's part. He knew that no one but she had seen the entities. That no one else had seen the physical evidence. Ms. Grumman was an ally, but she had never seen the two entities, and that kept a seed of doubt, which Milton was ready to exploit. How could Lynton prove there were two evil entities? She could not. Her word was all anyone had.

She walked around the church yard, hesitating, hovering; she reflected that she had already, with him, hurt herself beyond repair. Therefore she could patch up nothing. For the first minute since his arrival she wanted to get away from him. Now Lynton was probably the bravest woman in the Philippines, and she had faced many demons in the past and come out triumphant. However, the living demons were always the worst, and now she was coming face to face with a 10 year old demon. Milton was no longer just a little boy lost. He was a demon lost in the clutches of those two abominations.

Lynton thought that she might easily put an end to her horrifying predicament by getting away altogether, just giving up and walking away. Here was her chance; there was no one to stop her. She could give the whole thing up and tell Gordon Sanchez that if he wanted a story he'd have to find someone else.

LYNTON AND THE GHOSTS
AT THE MANSION ON BALETE DRIVE

No one, in short, could blame her if she should just drive desperately off. Yet, there was a hold the place had on her. She was never a quitter, and what of Flo? Even if Milton were irretrievably lost, was she?

It seemed to her that by the time she reached the house she had made up my mind she would flee. The Sunday stillness both of the approaches and of the interior, in which she met no one, fairly excited her with a sense of opportunity to be free of the place of despair. Were she to get off quickly, she could go without a scene, without a word. Tormented, in the hallway to her room, with difficulties and obstacles in her mind, she took a seat at the top of the staircase, suddenly collapsing there on the top step and then, with a revulsion, recalling that it was exactly in the darkness of a night filled with evil things, she had seen the spectre of the most horrible of women. At this she was able to straighten herself and walked to her room. But when she opened the door she saw seated at her own table in clear noonday light a person whom, without her previous experience, she should have taken at the first blush for some housemaid who might have stayed at home to look after the place and who, availing herself of rare relief from observation and of the study table and her computer, had applied herself to the considerable effort of an e-mail to her sweetheart. There was an effort in the way that, while her arms rested on the table, her hands with evident weariness supported her head; but at the moment Lynton took this in she had already become aware that, in spite of her entrance, her attitude strangely persisted. Then it was, with the very act of its announcing itself, that her identity flared up in a change of posture. She rose, not as if she had heard Lynton, but with an indescribable grand melancholy of indifference and detachment, and, within a dozen feet of Lynton, stood there letting out a low mournful cry.

Lynton was fixed at the creature in a dark as midnight black dress, and in her haggard beauty and her unutterable woe, she glanced at Lynton long enough to appear to say that her right to sit at the table was as good as hers. While these instants lasted, indeed, Lynton had the extraordinary chill of feeling that it was she who was the intruder.

The apparition looked at Lynton with evil intentions burned into its fiery eyes. Lynton blinked and there was nothing in the room the next minute but the sunshine and a sense that she must stay at the house on Balete Drive. She could not desert the children. She simply could not.

Looking out the window, she saw a lone figure stealing around the pond in a very clandestine manner. He was a young man, and definitely not an apparition.

LYNTON AND THE GHOSTS
AT THE MANSION ON BALETE DRIVE

She made her way to the gazebo area in search of the figure. She looked over at the old shed that was used to store materials and wondered if he had somehow gone in there. She saw the door was ajar. Moving cautiously, she slowly pushed it open. From behind her, a shove pushed her inside and she fell to the floor as the door was quickly closed. A voice demanded, "Are you one of them?"

Turning over, Lynton stared up at a young man in his early 20's, very handsome but seemingly haggard. "Am I one of them? One of what?"

He was breathing haltingly and said again, "Are you one of them?"

"My dear man, I have no idea what you mean."

Seemingly exhausted, he eased his back against the wall by the door and slowly moved downward into a sitting position. He put his face into his hands and began to cry.

Lynton, no longer fearful said, "Do not be afraid. I am just a poor governess here, and I will do you no harm."

He pointed over at the far wall where there was a trap door that was open. "The fiend put me in there, left me for dead."

LYNTON AND THE GHOSTS
AT THE MANSION ON BALETE DRIVE

Lynton walked over and looked down at an old root cellar. She then turned to him and said, "You were in there?"

"My cell phone would not work down there. For three weeks no less I survived eating bugs, roots and drank the disgusting water that seeped in from the pond."

"And who put you down here?"

"I do not know. I am a cub reporter for the Manila Herald."

Instantly, Lynton broke in, "Louis Benificio."

Shocked, he blurted out, "You know me?"

"I know Gordon Sanchez. That is why I am here, completing the job he thought you had deserted. You may know me. I am Lynton Viñas."

"Of course I know you. Gordon sent you here to get at the truth of what goes on here, then?"

"Yes, tell me what happened to you."

"I came back here without telling him. I wanted to gather up some photographic evidence, because I had seen nothing concrete, but had sensed a presence often. I was walking about the grounds in

J. Wayne Frye

hopes of finding some type of physical evidence. I saw this door ajar, came in, walked over to the trap door and suddenly from behind I was pushed. I screamed and hollered, but the earth is moist and absorbs all noise. I could not reach the door, and assumed I would die. Today, the earth was extremely wet from the afternoon rain that seeped into the walls of the hell hole I was in. I managed to carve out some steps up the wall with my hands, finally reaching the top and fortunately the door was never locked apparently."

"You have no idea who pushed you?"

"No, but a short person probably, because I was pushed from right above the tail bone, and there was something else. There was a giggle, an unusual giggle. Can't put my fingers on what it was like, but, yes, an unusual giggle."

"You stay here. I will leave the gate unlocked. Everyone will be asleep around midnight. Slip out then. Tell Gordon that things are coming to a head, and that all will be revealed soon." She started toward the door, looked down at his emaciated body and said, "I'll slip you some food and drink."

Lynton tried to figure what had happened, but there was no plausible explanation. Bewildered, she got Louis's food and brought it to him.

As he ravenously devoured the food, she said, "Could it have been a child that pushed you?"

"Maybe, yes."

"Can you give me the exact day when it happened?"

"Well, I have lost track of time, but it was maybe three weeks ago. I cannot be sure. I left Gordon's office and got an apartment near here, spent a few days planning my manoeuvres. Maybe it was on a Friday about three, no four weeks ago. Yeah, four weeks ago."

Lynton sighed and thought that it was a Friday when Milton returned from school. Could he have? Would he have?

Leaving Louis to make his escape in due time, Lynton returned to the house, secure in the knowledge that she was about to bring things to a head. The next day was uneventful but her two charges seemed less attentive, less affectionate toward her.

As the day drew to a close, Lynton found Ms. Grumman sitting in pained placidity in the kitchen. Sitting down across from her, she said, "Have you noticed the children are less affectionate today?"

LYNTON AND THE GHOSTS
AT THE MANSION ON BALETE DRIVE

"No, not at all. In fact, they seemed more affectionate to me than ever. They did mention they thought you would be leaving soon. Hope not, miss."

"No, I am not leaving. Did they say why I might be leaving? Milton and I had a very telling conversation. He knows I know now. So, he is a bit bewildered I am afraid. Also, I had a visitor to my room last night – a visitor with nefarious intentions."

"A visitor?"

"Ms. James."

"Oh my?'

"I found her at my computer table."

"Did she speak, miss?"

"No, but you could see what she wanted to say. She is tormented beyond belief."

.

"Yes ma'am. She is lost. She is damned."

"She wants Flo."

"Oh miss, no, please do not say that. Not that little innocent thing."

LYNTON AND THE GHOSTS
AT THE MANSION ON BALETE DRIVE

"I am going to have to call their uncle and let him know the dire circumstances we are experiencing here and recommend he get them away from this place."

"Oh, miss, please do. I fear he will be indifferent, but you must try."

"I shall tell him of the letter from the school. Oh, that will surely make him understand the urgency."

Having never shared the letter with Ms. Grumman, because she felt it inappropriate to share gossip, unfounded assertions, Ms. Grumman was in the dark about the letter, but said. "You have not shared it with me and I understand why. Is it really so abhorrent?"

"His uncle must know the reason he was expelled. He must know and maybe that will bring him here, bring him to help me rescue these two from evil."

Finally, Ms. Grumman could resist no longer. "Miss, I know you do not want to speak out of turn, and maybe I am not worthy to know, but please, I should know. I love the children too."

Nodding her head affirmatively, Lynton said, "Wickedness!"

J. Wayne Frye

LYNTON AND THE GHOSTS
AT THE MANSION ON BALETE DRIVE

"What?"

"For wickedness. For what else, when he's so clever and beautiful and perfect? Is he stupid? Is he untidy? Is he infirm? Is he ill-natured? He's exquisite, so it can be only that. Nothing is spelled out in the letter, nothing is overtly said, it only reads 'expelled for reasons of impropriety and inappropriate behaviour toward his classmates, the facility and the administration."

"My miss."

"I partly blame their uncle for being so inattentive to their needs."

"My fault too miss. Perhaps I should have been more observant, more open about what Quincy and Ms. James were doing."

"Do not blame yourself. You are a victim of circumstances as are the children. I shall write him an e-mail tonight, but I must compose myself and think exactly how I am going to reveal all that has occurred to him."

Bowing her head, Ms. Grumman took a deep breath and said, "Yes miss, do as you must for the sake of the children. I am so upset about all that has occurred. Isn't it funny though that the apparitions only appeared when you came."

LYNTON AND THE GHOSTS
AT THE MANSION ON BALETE DRIVE

There was almost a note of disrespect in that comment. It was if Ms. Grumman was somehow questioning whether Lynton was the catalyst that caused the apparitions. Lynton reflected on the comment as she walked away, but remembered there were previous manifestations of questionable occurrences when Louis Benificio was there for a brief time. Though he had not seen the ghosts directly, he felt their presence, sensed there was something amiss. The more Lynton thought about that comment the more indignant she became. How dare Ms. Grumman question my veracity she thought?

J. Wayne Frye

CHAPTER 12
SHE IS NOT ALONE

The weather had changed back, as a typhoon was brewing in the Pacific. Great wind was abroad, and the shutters had been pulled closed. Lynton sat for a long time staring at her computer screen listening to the lash of the rain and the batter of the gusts. Finally she went out, taking a flash light rather than turning on the lights. She stopped and listened a minute at Milton's door. What, under her endless obsession, she had been impelled to listen for was some betrayal of his not being at rest. Then, she heard his voice. "I say, you there come in."

She walked in, not turning on the light but standing there with her flashlight focusing on Milton lying in bed. "Well, what are you up to?" he asked with a grace of sociability.

She stood there staring. "How did you know I was there?"

"I heard you of course. Your little trickery of tiptoeing and not turning on any lights does not fool me."

"Then you weren't asleep?'"

"Not much! I lie awake and think. I think a lot."

LYNTON AND THE GHOSTS
AT THE MANSION ON BALETE DRIVE

She moved next to his bed, and the room was still dark except for the very dim light given off by the flashlight. "And what is it that you think of so much?"

"Why you my dear. What else? Why you are in a frightful state aren't you? Yes, you are always in a frightful state. My, my, you seem to be going over the edge psychologically don't you think? I think you need a long rest, very long. I believe you are just having a frightful time with this unusual business of ours."

"What unusual business?"

He lay silent for awhile, just staring into her eyes. Finally he said, "Oh, we need not broach the subject. You know of what business I speak."

Lynton could say nothing for a minute, though she felt that the boy was thoroughly enjoying playing a game of cat and mouse. Finally, she broke the silence. "Milton, we must get to the bottom of something."

"Oh yes, we must or you will simply bust won't you?"

"Do you know you've never said a word to me about your school and the reason you were expelled?"

LYNTON AND THE GHOSTS
AT THE MANSION ON BALETE DRIVE

"Haven't I?"

Something in his tone and the expression of his face set her heart racing. He was playing with her. She said, "Never - from the hour you came back have you uttered a word about the expulsion. You've never mentioned to me one of your teachers, one of your fellow students, nor the least little about anything that happened to you at school. Therefore you can fancy how much I'm in the dark. Not since that incident at the terminal have you scarce even made a reference to anything in your previous life. It is as if there is something you want to avoid."

Suddenly, he blurted out, "You are a good person and want to help me. I can't be helped, though."

"I try to be good Milton. I try very hard, and no one is beyond help, absolutely no one."

"Maybe."

She looked over at his nightstand and noticed something strange. There, resting on the table was a hammer. What was he doing with a hammer? She let it go, as she thought perhaps it was something he felt he needed to defend himself with if that abomination Quincy showed up in the middle of the night.

LYNTON AND THE GHOSTS
AT THE MANSION ON BALETE DRIVE

"You are telling my uncle of all this are you not?"

"He needs to come here Milton and take you and your sister away. You know why?"

"Do I? Does she? Does anyone really know why?"

"Will you tell him all? Tell him what you have not shared with me? There are things you will have to tell him."

"What things?"

"The things you've never told me."

Then he said with determined serenity, with positive unimpeachable forcefulness in a most unnatural tragic voice, "If you only knew. If you only knew the depth of depravity."

Lynton was overwhelmed with emotion and threw herself onto the bed, grabbing him and pulling him to her breast as she was surging with pity for the poor lost soul. "Dear Milton, my dear Milton."

Her face was close to his, and she lightly kissed him on the cheek as she, in a tearful voice said, "I'll make it alright."

LYNTON AND THE GHOSTS
AT THE MANSION ON BALETE DRIVE

He pulled her closer to him. The moment was tender, but the tenderness was short-lived as she said, "Is there nothing, nothing at all that you want to tell me?"

He turned facing around toward the wall and whispered. "I've told you."

"That you just want me not to worry about you?"

Then he became very cold and indifferent. "To just leave me alone."

There was no love in his answer, rather insolent disrespect. Lynton stood up, looked down at him speechless.

He looked at her harshly. "You can contact my uncle all you want. He doesn't care. He is indifferent to our plight."

"Maybe he is indifferent, but he may not be as heartless as you think. Tell me Milton, what happened before?"

"Before what?"

"Before you came back. And before you went away, too. I want to know everything, only then can I really help you."

LYNTON AND THE GHOSTS
AT THE MANSION ON BALETE DRIVE

For some time he was silent, but he continued to meet her eyes. "What happened?"

For the first time, Lynton felt some conscious fear on his part. "Yes my dear boy. I need to know. You see, I want to help you. I want to save you, but I can only do it with your help."

Suddenly, she knew she had gone too far. The answer to her appeal was instantaneous, but it came in the form of an extraordinary blast and chill, a gust of frozen air, and a shake of the room as great as if the wild wind had roared in from the outside. He gave a loud, high shriek, an exhortation of terror.

She jumped to her feet again and was conscious of complete darkness as her flashlight had completely faded. So for a moment they remained, while she stared about her and saw that the drawn curtains across the way were moving. She looked down and saw some work shoes sticking out from under them. She said nothing as she just looked down at Milton who, looking up at her in coldness said, "We have nothing to talk about. Out of my room please so I can sleep."

Lynton did not move toward the curtains, but she knew what was behind them. She was not ready to confront Quincy face-to-face until the advantage was hers.

LYNTON AND THE GHOSTS
AT THE MANSION ON BALETE DRIVE

The next day, after lessons, Mrs. Grumman said, "Did you write the e-mail?"

"I did," Lynton replied, but she did not add that she had not sent it. Yes, it was written, but somehow she was reluctant to send it for fear that his indifference would simply make her job more difficult. Anyway, she was stubbornly independent and determined to see this through.

The morning with the children was exemplary, and no mention was made by little Milton of the previous night's strange occurrence. Still, there was a dark pall over the happiness, as lingering beneath the surface was the evil that had wrapped itself around each one of them in one way or another.

Milton, near dinner time, came around to Lynton and asked if they might play chess. As he moved a knight into a defensive position, Milton said, "The true knights we love to read about never push an advantage too far. I know what you mean now; you mean if I act a certain way, you'll cease to worry and spy upon me, won't keep me so close to you, will let me go and come. Well, I come, you see, but I don't go!"

She knew what he was talking about. He meant that like Quincy he was trapped by circumstances in a state of limbo.

LYNTON AND THE GHOSTS
AT THE MANSION ON BALETE DRIVE

Milton got up from the chess table, game not over, and walked over to the piano, sat down and began to play Moonlight Sonata. As he skilfully played, Lynton looked at him and wondered just what she could do. Why did she not write the uncle, she asked herself? The answer was more than his indifference. She sensed that he would not believe her about the apparitions. After all, who had seen them for sure? Her, Milton and Flo were it. Ms. Grumman had seen evidence, but not the actual apparitions.

Lost in the beauty of Milton's playing, she began to wonder where Flo was. She had not seen her in at least an hour. When she put the question in regards to her whereabouts to Milton, he played on a minute before answering and then could only dismissively say: "Why, my dear, how should I know?"

Lynton went straight to Flo's room, but she was not there; then, before going downstairs, she looked into several other rooms to no avail. As she was nowhere about she would surely be with Ms. Grumman assumed Lynton. No luck there either. So, she and Ms. Grumman began a fevered search. They split up and went about the house. Fifteen minutes later they met in the hall, only to report on either side that after guarded inquiries they had altogether failed to trace her. They exchanged mute alarms.

J. Wayne Frye

LYNTON AND THE GHOSTS
AT THE MANSION ON BALETE DRIVE

.   Ms. Grumman said, "We must go to the top floor and search again. Surely that is where she is."

Lynton, very assuredly, said, "No, she is not in the house. She is with her?"

"Her?"

"Ms. James."

"Oh my miss."

"We must find them."

The piano playing had been stopped for some time. Lynton said, "And he has gone to be with him."

"Miss, what are you saying?"

"I am saying I know that the end is at hand. Those abominations are about to make their move. Never mind Milton at this point. He, I fear is closer to being lost than Flo, maybe he is already irretrievably lost. Come, we must rescue Flo from the clutches of that thing."

"Sweet Jesus, ma'am, we need to pray."

"No, we need to act."

LYNTON AND THE GHOSTS
AT THE MANSION ON BALETE DRIVE

"What are we to do? We need the Lord's help."

Lynton, never one to make fun of the poor souls who clung to religion because that is all they had in a life filled with want – the hope that after death they would have all they were denied in life – did not admonish her. She only said, "Right now is not the time for prayer. Now is the time for action. This is all part of an elaborate plan. Milton found the most divine little way to keep me occupied while she went off to be with her."

"But what of Milton ma'am, is he not in danger too? Should we not be concerned with him as we are with her?"

"He is in mortal danger, yes. His danger is very real and perhaps more substantial. However, his danger is maybe now beyond rescue. Right now, we must save Flo."

The storm of the night and the early morning had dropped, but the afternoon was damp and grey. The two women forged toward the pond, because Lynton knew where the rendezvous would occur. They went straight toward the pond. Ms. Grumman hurried trying to keep up with the nearly running Lynton.

"You're going to the pond miss? You believe that is where she will be?"

"I do. That is where the two of them convened before. I judge it most likely that she's on the spot from which, the other day, we saw together what I told you."

"When she pretended not to see?"

"With that astounding self-possession? I've always been sure she wanted to go back alone. And now her brother has managed it for her."

"You suppose they actually talk to those abominations?"

"Oh, they talk to them alright. They say things that, if we heard them, would simply appal us with their wickedness."

"And if she is there?"

"Oh, she is there. I assure you."

Lynton was so quick in her strides that Ms. Grumman simply could not keep up, but Lynton could not tarry as she knew that time was of the essence. On the way, she passed the shed where she had met Louis Benificio, and she noticed the door was slightly ajar. He must have left it open when he sneaked off the grounds she thought - foolish, but understandable that he would forget to close it in his haste.

LYNTON AND THE GHOSTS
AT THE MANSION ON BALETE DRIVE

By the time she reached the pond, Ms. Grumman was huffing and panting, close behind her she exhaled a moan of relief as they at last came in sight of the greater part of the water without a sight of the child. There was no trace of Flo on that nearer side of the bank where Lynton's observation of her had been most startling, and none on the opposite edge, where, save for a margin of some twenty feet, a thick fog clung over the water. The pond, oblong in shape, had a width so scant compared to its length that, with its ends out of view, it might have been taken for a small lake. They looked at the empty expanse, and then Lynton noticed the boat was missing.

"The boat, she has taken the boat out."

"Perhaps she has, but why would it not be on the far shore."

Knowing the sinister nature of the children, Lynton replied, "She hid it."

"Oh my, the child is out there all alone."

Lynton looked her straight in the eyes and said, "Oh no. She is not alone.

J. Wayne Frye

CHAPTER 13
SOMEHOW SAVE MILTON

Lynton scanned all the visible shore realizing that the boat might be in a small refuge formed by one of the recesses of the pond, an indentation masked, for the hither side, by a projection of the bank and by a clump of trees growing close to the water. She squinted her eyes and sure enough there it was. You could just see the hull just slightly under a tree branch. She pointed it out to Ms. Grumman.

For some reason, Lynton turned her attention to the shed door that had been left ajar. She turned to Ms. Grumman and said, "Keep an eye on the distant shore. I am going to investigate the shed."

"The shed? But she could not be in there miss."

"No, but why is the door ajar?"

"I am sure I don't know miss. Yes, take a look."

Lynton very cautiously moved toward the shed. The door was only half ajar, and she very slowly pushed it all the way open and walked in. Nothing was out place. She walked over to the place where the trap door was and looked down. Nothing there. Then she turned to go back to the door and on her left she saw it. She stood there unable to move.

LYNTON AND THE GHOSTS
AT THE MANSION ON BALETE DRIVE

In the far corner, sticking out from behind a large box was a pair of legs. She instantly recognized the pants. She walked over and there he was. Louis Benificio never made it back to the newspaper. She bent down, looking at the huge hole in his head. He had, no doubt, been felled with one well-delivered deadly blow to the back of his skull. He had obviously been dead for some time based upon the coagulated blood on the wound and the dried blood on the floor. The indentation on the head was evidence enough of what instrument had been used to kill him. Yes, it was a hammer.

Not showing any emotion, she closed and latched the door. There would be time enough later to call the police, because Louis was obviously going nowhere, nor was his killer. What counted now was finding Flo.

Ms. Grumman said, "Anything in there?"

Not wanting to alarm her, Lynton replied, "No, nothing at all."

Lynton looked long and hard at Ms. Grumman. So long and so hard that Ms. Grumman felt uncomfortable. "What is it?" she said.

The wheels were spinning now in Lynton's head as she said, "I have a question."

LYNTON AND THE GHOSTS
AT THE MANSION ON BALETE DRIVE

"Yes ma'am?"

"You said Quincy apparently passed out from drunkenness, but that he had his head bashed in, right?"

"Yes ma'am. It was just one nasty blow apparently to his skull. Killed him it did."

"They ever postulate on what was used to deliver the blow?"

"Yes ma'am, I already told you they said it was probably a hammer. Strange thing for someone to be carrying around in the dead of night. Of course, as I said, the culprit was never caught. Don't think the police really cared much based on Quincy's reputation. They simply thought one of his many enemies must have decided it was a good time to get rid of him."

"My guess is that the murder was committed by someone he knew very well, someone who lived nearby and was able to easily get the weapon when he observed Quincy passed out. But that is not our concern at this time. We must find Flo or she is lost forever."

"We must walk around to the far end of the pond. It will take us a few minutes. We must hurry."

LYNTON AND THE GHOSTS
AT THE MANSION ON BALETE DRIVE

Ms. Grumman dragged at her heels, and when they had gotten halfway around, a tiresome process, on ground much broken and by a path choked with overgrowth, they were breathing heavily. The rested a few seconds and then started walking again until they reached a point from which they found the boat. It had been intentionally left as much as possible out of sight. Lynton recognized, as she looked at the pair of short, thick oars, quite safely drawn up, the prodigious character of the feat for a little girl. There was a fence nearby and they walked over to the gate in the fence, through which they passed, and that brought them, after a trifling interval, more into the open. Then, there she was.

Flo, a short way off, stood before them in the nearby clearing. She waited for Lynton and Ms. Grumman, almost as if she were expecting them. As the two women approached her, she smiled but there was an ominous silence that permeated all about. Not even the birds were chirping nor was there even a rustle of any leaves. Ms. Grumman was the first to break the spell. She threw herself on her knees and, drawing the child to her breast, clasped in a long embrace the little tender, yielding body. While this convulsion of affection was occurring, Lynton surveyed the scene, for she knew that there must be another party around. Flo's face peeped at her over Ms. Grumman's shoulder. It was a sinisterly serious look now, the

J. Wayne Frye

kind that sent chills up and down the spine. The little eyes flickered and the mouth slowly let an evil grin stretch across it.

When Ms. Grumman slowly rose, holding the child's hand, Lynton saw in that once angelic face the bitterness of someone who no longer was in possession of their faculties. She was now possessed.

Still, not a word was spoken. Then suddenly Flo said with an earnest tone, "Where is Milton?"

There was something in the small valour of it that quite finished Lynton. Those three words from her were, in a flash like the glitter of a drawn blade, the jostle of the cup of hope had crashed to the ground.

"I'll tell you where he is if you will tell me where someone is. Where is Ms. James?"

She was getting seemingly agitated now as all she did was stare, until after a few seconds she blurted out, "She is dead, of course, you stupid bitch. She is among the worms. That is where she is. You know that you imbecile."

For some reason, without explanation, Ms. Grumman seemed to turn on Lynton. "Don't torment the child."

LYNTON AND THE GHOSTS
AT THE MANSION ON BALETE DRIVE

"Torment?"

"Yes, can't you see she is frightened?"

"Oh no, she is not frightened at all are you Flo?"

In a dismissive, arrogant tone, Flo replied, "Why, what is it that you expect of me, bitch."

So, the transformation was complete. Her little soul had been conquered by evil. Meanwhile, as Ms. Grumman stood still holding her hand, she looked down at Flo in astonishment that words of nastiness could come from the mouth of such a sweet child. Ms. Grumman then looked up at Lynton, almost pleading in her manner for Lynton somehow to save them all from the horrid situation. As Ms. Grumman looked in bewilderment at Lynton, something came into view across the nearby path in the distance. The fog obscured Lynton's vision, but the outline became very clear. It was the proof of evil. She was there, and Lynton was justified; she was there. She was there for poor scared Ms. Grumman to turn and see for the first time, but she was there most for Flo; and no moment of the monstrous time was perhaps so extraordinary as that in which Lynton consciously threw out to Ms. Grumman a plea that was uttered very quietly: "Turn Ms. Grumman very slowly and behold the evil that has captured this child's soul."

J. Wayne Frye

LYNTON AND THE GHOSTS
AT THE MANSION ON BALETE DRIVE

The apparition was very slowly disappearing now. This first vividness of vision and emotion were things of a few seconds, during which Ms. Grumman's dazed blink across to where Lynton pointed struck as a sovereign sign that she too at last saw the evil before all. The revelation then of the manner in which Flo was affected startled Lynton. Flo had collapsed into Ms. Grumman's arms. As she did, Lynton cried, "There, gaze upon that abomination." Then she moved to Flo, grabbed her and turned her toward the apparition saying, "Look upon her and deny her. Deny the evil and save your soul little one."

Ms. Grumman was now squinting, trying to focus. She said, "It is only an outline in the fog, miss. I cannot see an image of Ms. James. It is the fog playing tricks upon you. That is all."

She grasped Ms. Grumman now as she pointed, for even while she spoke the hideous plain presence stood outlined in the distance undimmed and undaunted. It had already lasted a minute, and it lasted while Lynton continued, seizing her colleague, pleading with her to focus and see.

As she was pleading with Ms. Grumman to open her eyes and see the truth, Little Flo looked around Ms. Grumman's side up at Lynton, staring at her intently with eyes that glinted with evil intentions. She was smiling now.

LYNTON AND THE GHOSTS
AT THE MANSION ON BALETE DRIVE

Still, Ms. Grumman looked, but with a deep groan of negation, repulsion, compassion, that seemed to mix with her relief at her exemption from belief that there was an apparition there in the distance. Now, Lynton could make out a faint smile on the apparition's lips.

All the while, Flo just stared at the now frantic Lynton, who was realizing that the apparitions only appeared to those who possessed that special power of being able to see that which normal people could not see.

"She isn't there, and nobody's there and you never see anything, my dear! How can poor Ms. James be there if she is dead and buried?" She took the child by the hand and looked at Lynton with pity as she said, "Come miss. We will all go back to the house and get some rest. Yes, a good rest will help you. Help us all."

And all the while, Flo was looking up at Lynton, almost saying, though completely silent, "See, no one will believe you, absolutely no one. We have won the day. You have lost."

Lynton could say nothing. She stood in silence thinking of the murdered Benificio, but there was no need to tell Ms. Grumman of the hammer that was beside Milton's bed and was obviously the murder weapon. Also, it was the same weapon that

J. Wayne Frye

had, no doubt, dispatched Quincy the night he lay in a drunken stupor passed out and easy prey for a little boy.

Finally, Ms. Grumman, as they started back, turned indignant. "I don't know what you mean by doing all this, miss. I saw nobody. I saw nothing. I never have. I think you're cruel. I don't like you!"

Then, after this deliverance, Flo squeezed Ms. Grumman's hand tighter and looked up smiling at Lynton, making sure that Ms. Grumman could not see her. She screamed to Ms. Grumman, "Take me from this evil woman, please. She wants to hurt me."

Ms. Grumman looked across at Lynton dismayed, as Lynton looked back one last time into the fog and there Ms. James was, waving her hand and smiling with a sense of victory burned into her face. She said nothing to Ms. Grumman. What was the point? She could not see the apparition. She had nothing to do but communicate a forlorn acknowledgement that victory belonged to evil. The wretched child had spoken exactly as if she had got from some outside source each of her stabbing little words, and Lynton, therefore, in the full despair of all had to accept the circumstance. This was not the outcome that usually occurred with the dynamic dynamo. She was never defeated. She never quit.

LYNTON AND THE GHOSTS
AT THE MANSION ON BALETE DRIVE

Lynton, never one to admit defeat, this time felt she had lost. Evil was triumphant. As they walked back to the house, she looked over at Flo and said, "I know what is inside you, and I, for the first time, must admit defeat at the hands of evil. I did my best, but I have lost you." She then walked away from the two, hurrying toward the house in hopes she might somehow save Milton.

J. Wayne Frye

CHAPTER 14
YOU SEE WHAT OTHERS DO NOT

On reaching the house, Lynton paused a moment as coming down the stars was Milton. He stood and looked at her without speaking. She walked into the study and sank into a chair. He walked in and took a seat across from her, and they sat in silence as Flo and Ms. Grumman came in and went upstairs without any acknowledgement.

Milton lowered his head and finally spoke, but did not look at her as he did. "I am not all evil you know?"

"I know that Milton. I know much more than you think I do."

"Do you?"

"Oh, I do indeed."

"I think you want to give me an opening. Last evening, we sat here in this very room and I sensed you wanted to share something with me. You know this is not America. Children are not executed here. They are not locked up for life when they commit a crime. I have waited and waited for you to breach the silence of what is going on. You know your sister is now in a frightful condition and you know what caused it."

He got up and walked out without as much as another word. As he left, Ms. Grumman walked in. Lynton felt so alone now, as she apparently had lost her friend. She said, "I'll go if you insist, but I don't want to."

"Miss, there is a change in my opinion now."

"You mean that you have seen?"

She shook her head vehemently "I've heard."

"Heard?"

"From that child. Heard of horrors," she sighed with tragic relief. "On my honour, miss, she says such things." But at this evocation she broke down; she dropped, with a sudden sob, upon her knees by the sofa.

"Then we are in concord again?"

She immediately stood up and said, "We are." Without hesitation, she continued, "She's so horrible."

Lynton saw her colleague scarce knew how to put it. "Really shocking what she is revealing."

"Oh my, miss, I cannot believe the words that come out of that little innocent mouth."

LYNTON AND THE GHOSTS
AT THE MANSION ON BALETE DRIVE

"And what does she say of me?"

"About you, miss, since you must have it. It's beyond everything, for a young lady; and I can't think wherever she must have picked up the awful words she uses to describe you."

"Oh, I know from whence those words come, believe me."

"The appalling language she applied even to me?"

"Maybe she is not lost after all. Maybe there is a transition period that we can counter somehow. I am so relieved that you believe now. I felt so alone."

"I believe miss. I do. I am sorry that I doubted you."

Smiling, Lynton got up and embraced her. "My dear, I was beginning to doubt myself."

It was a joy that they were still shoulder to shoulder in the battle. Lynton said, "It strikes me that by this time your eyes are open even wider than mine."

They proved to be so indeed, but she could still blush. "I make out now what he must have done at school miss," said the humbled Ms, Grumman And she gave, in her simple sharpness, an almost droll disillusioned nod. "He stole."

Not wanting to burden her too much, Lynton just said, "Well, maybe."

The dear woman kissed Lynton on the cheek and through tears said, "You are a good woman trying to save those two poor souls from damnation. I am here to help you anyway I can. Go, if you will, and minister to Milton, and keep him close to you. He is fraught with anger but you are his only hope to save him from damnation.

Lynton made her way upstairs and she pushed open his door only to find him gone. She walked over to his desk and picked up the hammer, realizing that she had just put her hands on a murder weapon and left fingerprints. She walked back to her room, looked around and wondered where she could put it. She would have to call the police about the body soon, as it would begin to smell abysmally and someone would eventually discover it. Then, she realized where to put the hammer and keep it from prying eyes. Milton had gone out for a stroll, so she would look for him and at the same time take the hammer down to the pond and toss it in. Yes, she was shielding Quincy's murderer, but the little killer was, no doubt, driven by the evil perpetrated against him.

J. Wayne Frye

LYNTON AND THE GHOSTS
AT THE MANSION ON BALETE DRIVE

On the other hand, there was the murder of Benificio, which she chalked up to Milton being possessed by the evil spirit of Quincy. She walked to the pond with great trepidation, trying to figure out her next move. She thought that if so much had sprung to the surface, she could scarce put it too strongly in saying that what had perhaps sprung highest was the absurdity of she and Milton prolonging the fiction of what was going on.

The time for playing coy games was past. Here at present she felt afresh, for she had felt it again and again how her equilibrium depended on the success of her rigid will to fight the evil, the will to face the truth of what she had to deal with. She was prepared to tackle her monstrous ordeal as a push in a direction unusual, unpleasant, demanding, but with a possibility of success now.

Finding Milton by the pond, she sensed that he had seen her toss away the hammer. In silence, they shared their solitude, and they then began to frolic about the pond and broke out with a specious glitter of joy in each others company. She felt an overpowering urge to save him from the evil of the place. She thought that mightn't one, to reach his mind, risk the stretch of an angular arm over his character? It was as if, when they were face to face in the dining room after they went into the house, he had literally shown

J. Wayne Frye   187

her the way to rescue him. She began to genuinely feel that if she rescued him, she would free Flo too, because Ms. James was an adjunct of Quincy. Free Milton of Quincy's influence and you would free Flo too, because without Quincy Ms. James had no power.

Flo had her dinner in her room and Milton and Lynton were in the dining room eating when he said to her, "I say, my dear, is Flo really very awfully ill?"

"Little Flo? Not so bad that she will not presently be better. She just had a bad experience today. Want to know about it."

"Oh, I know what happened. It was dreadful, but you know it was brought on because of you."

"You mean it is my fault that she is seeing things."

"It is you, my dear, who are seeing things."

Not wanting to press him too much, she said. "Oh."

He was irreproachable, as always, but he was unmistakably more conscious. He was discernibly trying to take for granted more things than he found, without assistance, quite easy; and he dropped into peaceful silence while he considered his situation. Their meal was brief.

Milton got up, walked over to the window where Lynton had seen the manifestation of Quincy the second time. Milton looked out into the darkness. No words were exchanged but finally Milton, almost as delivering a soliloquy, recited a poem.

> *Day shifts into day*
> *Mortals fall away*
> *Creature of the night*
> *In its longfull flight*
> *Madness overtaking*
> *Insanity not mistaking*
> *Power in the night*
> *Creeps away in fright*
> *Fearful of insanity's bite*
> *Evil is master of the night*

While reciting, Milton stood with his hands in his little pockets and his back to Lynton, stood and looked out of the wide window through which, that other day, Lynton had seen the very embodiment of evil. After he recited, the two continued silent while the maid cleared the table, also in silence. It whimsically occurred to Lynton that the two were like some young couple who, on their first intimate night, at an inn, feel shy in the presence of each other. He turned around only when the maid left. "Well, so we're alone!"

"Oh, more or less. Not absolutely."
.

"No, I suppose we are never completely alone in this place."

"Well, the maid is gone to the kitchen, and Flo and Ms. Grumman are upstairs, so we are sort of alone here in this room."

"Oh, my dear, you know that even if they were all gone from the house that we would still not be alone."

Lynton felt he was beginning to open up. "What do you mean?"

"We have others here with us."

"We have the others with us. We have indeed the others," she replied with firm assurance.

"Yet even though we have them," he retorted still with his hands in his pockets and planted there in front of her now as he had moved away from the window, "they don't much count, do they?"

"It depends on what you call much."

"Yes, everything depends!" On this, however, he faced to the window again and presently reached it with his vague, restless, cogitating step. He remained there awhile, with his forehead against the glass, in contemplation of the darkness.

An extraordinary impression dropped on her as she extracted a meaning from staring at the boy's back, none other than the impression that she was suddenly barred now from him as he was in deep contemplation. This inference grew in a few minutes to sharp intensity and seemed bound up with the direct perception that he was somehow communing with the darkness outside.

The frames and squares of the huge window were a kind of image, for him, reflecting his failure to beat Quincy. She felt deep hurt for him and thought him a boy lost to evil who was trying to fight it. She took it in with a throb of hope. Wasn't he looking, through the haunted pane, for something he couldn't see? Wasn't it the first instance in the whole time there that he was facing up to what was happening?

When he at last turned around, he said as he walked to the dining room table, "Well, I think I am lost. Do you?"

"No, not at all. You are good Milton. Yes, a good boy put in bad circumstances."

He bowed his head and took a seat. "I am not good."

LYNTON AND THE GHOSTS
AT THE MANSION ON BALETE DRIVE

"We all do things that we are ashamed of, and sometimes it is so bad we cannot deal with it unless we get professional help. No matter what you have done, there is still hope for you."

He looked at her more directly, and the expression of his face, graver now, struck Lynton as, for the first time, showing a little boy who was scared. "You are staying here just for me aren't you?"

"And Flo. I stay on as your friend and from the tremendous interest I take in your welfare." Her voice trembled as she continued, "Don't you remember how I told you, when I came and sat on your bed that night, that there was nothing in the world I wouldn't do for you?"

"Yes, yes!" He, more and more visibly nervous, said, "Only that, I think, was to get me to do something for you."

"But, you know, you didn't do it."

"Oh, yes," he said with the brightest superficial eagerness, "you wanted me to tell you something."

"That's right."

"Ah, then, that is what keeps you here isn't it. You want to know."

LYNTON AND THE GHOSTS
AT THE MANSION ON BALETE DRIVE

He spoke with a quiver of resentful passion; but there was a note of surrender in his voice. It was as if what Lynton had worked for so long had come at last only to astonish her. "Well, yes, I may as well make a clean breast of it, it was precisely for that."

He waited so long that she supposed it for the purpose of repudiating the assumption on which her action had been founded; but what he finally said was "Do you mean now, here?"

"There couldn't be a better place or time."

He looked around uneasily. It was as if he were suddenly completely different. He was just a little boy now. Again he stared out the window. "I need some air. I feel it is stuffy in here."

"Go then. I will wait her for you," she said, thinking that giving him time to think would make him open up.

He smiled at her, picked up a piece of candy from the bowl on the dining cabinet and began to twirl it in his right hand, not taking the wrapper off. There seemed a perverse horror in what he was doing. You could see the guilt building up within him. He needed to unburden himself, but she did not want to rush it, though time was working against them.

LYNTON AND THE GHOSTS
AT THE MANSION ON BALETE DRIVE

She was now reading into their situation a clearness, for she seemed to see their eyes already lighted with some spark of a prevision of what was to come.

So they circled about like two fighters feeling each other out in the first round. They were cautious. He didn't really want to go outside. He wanted to unburden his tremendous quilt. Still, she wanted it to come from him, not be forced.

"I'll tell you everything," Milton said. "I mean I'll tell you anything you like. You'll stay on with me, and we shall both be all right, and I will tell you. I will. But not now, please."

"Why not now?"

Her insistence turned him from her and kept him once more at the window in a silence during which, between them, you might have heard a pin drop. Then he was before her again with the air of a person for whom, outside, someone who had frankly to be reckoned with was waiting. "I have to go outside."

"Can you tell me why you need to go outside?"

"Oh my dear, that you know, you see what others do not."

J. Wayne Frye

LYNTON AND THE GHOSTS
AT THE MANSION ON BALETE DRIVE

CHAPTER 15
LIFE HAD GONE FROM HIM

She hesitated, for she feared what was out there, but he had to face his fears. Only then could he defeat Quincy once and for all and she felt he was almost there, almost ready to unburden himself of all the pain he had carried for so long. "Well, then, go. I'll wait for what you promise. Only, in return for that, satisfy, before you leave me, one very much smaller request. Can you at least do that?"

He looked as if he felt he had succeeded enough to be able still to bargain. "Very much smaller?"

"Yes, a mere fraction of the whole. Tell me what you were looking at that night in the yard. Be honest – the truth."

Finally, he said it. "Quincy."

As he said that, she felt a surge of euphoric relief. Finally, she had reached him. Then, in full view with all his evil seeming to be pulsating from those piercing eyes that were peering into the dining room from the darkness that engulfed him Quincy was standing there, not against the window, but maybe three or four feet from it. He had been shielded from view by Milton's position between her and the window, but he was in full view now.

LYNTON AND THE GHOSTS
AT THE MANSION ON BALETE DRIVE

Quincy slowly moved toward the window, not walking but seemingly gliding, floating as it were. He was now at the window. Glaring in, he once more offered to the room his horrid face of damnation. At the sight, Lynton's decision was made. Frightened yes, but scared to inaction no. It came to her in the very horror of the immediate presence that the sanest act would be, seeing and facing what she saw and faced, to keep the boy himself unaware.

Milton suddenly turned his head toward the window as Lynton shouted, "No dear one. No, do not look."

The boy breathing like a long distance runner who had just finished a race, overwhelmed with fiery emotion, stared intently at the window, not so much in horror as much as hatred. Now, by Quincy's side, looking menacingly into the room was Ms. James.

Milton bolted from the room, running into the foyer and struggled to open the door. Lynton followed, reached for him just as he opened the door, missing him, bumping into the door and falling to the floor as he ran screaming into the darkness as she shouted, "No, don't go."

She struggled to her feet, running around to the side of the house where she saw Milton standing there shivering before a floating Quincy with Ms. James now by his side hovering over them like foul birds of prey searching for victims of their depravity.

The two apparitions had grown to grotesque proportions, floating precipitously above them. Milton just stood there, shaking with fear. For the first time he seemed genuinely human, capable of emotion. He was now shouting at the apparition. "I killed you devil, killed you with a blow from a hammer, but you will not die and disappear. You made me do evil things. You made me set my roommate's bed on fire, trying to kill him, trying to make me do anything to return here to embrace your evil. Take me you damnable abomination from the fiery pits of hell. I give in and bow before your evil. Take me! Take me!"

Lynton's sense of love and need to protect him surged into every fiber of her being as a fierce longing to hug him, to shield him from the evil overwhelmed her. She sprang to his side, drew him close, and wrapped her arms tightly around him, hiding his eyes from seeing the two manifestations of pure evil. Despite sharing his fear, her motherly instincts motivated an intense desire to protect him.

She was now fighting with a demon for a human soul, and when she had fairly so appraised it she saw how the human soul held out resting comfortably in her arms and for the first time showing genuine emotions, as he was crying uncontrollably, sobbing in her arms like a little baby. Finally she had broken through and found the real Milton deep within.

Through his tears he sobbed, "I love you."

At this, with a moan of joy, she drew him closer; and while she held him to her breast, where she could feel in the sudden fever of his little body the tremendous pulse of his little heart, she kept her eyes on the thing above her and saw it move and shift its posture. It was like a sentinel from hell waiting to bring another victim to damnation. The glare of the face was growing more grotesque, the scoundrel fixed intently on the two of them.

Suddenly, to their immediate left, and above, standing on the balcony, appeared Flo and she stood as in a trance glaring at Ms. James who had turned her floating body toward the lovely little girl. Lynton shouted, "Do not look darling girl. Do not look."

Flo could not help but look. She did not have the power to stand against the evil. She steadily, and with eyes focused on Ms. James, crawled onto the railing, finally standing precariously teetering back and forth.

J. Wayne Frye

LYNTON AND THE GHOSTS
AT THE MANSION ON BALETE DRIVE

Lynton's eyes were now focused on the two apparitions as she kept glancing out the side of her left eye at Flo. She pleaded with the evil entities. "Take me, not the children. Take me!"

Quincy had a smirk on his face. On Milton's own face, was the collapse of hope which showed how complete was the ravage of uneasiness. Yet, he almost smiled at her in the desolation of his surrender to Quincy's evil, which was indeed practically, by this time, so complete that the mighty demon fighter felt inadequate in his defence.

She let her grip on him go a little, as she looked up at Flo, still teetering on the railing. Again, she pleaded with both of the frightful apparitions. "Take me I tell you. Take me you damned abominations."

After Lynton's pleading, after a second in which Quincy's head made a jerking movement, the air around them become lighter and Milton gave a frantic little shake for breath as he collapsed in Lynton's arms and uttered, "I am done."

Ms. James, hovering to Quincy's left, began to beckon Flo with her right hand, urging her off the railing. Flo, as in slow motion, leaned forward and tumbled off the balcony, her little body plunging downward onto the stone pavement, landing with a thud. Lynton's heart nearly stopped as tears filled her eyes.

A sinister grin crept across Ms. James' lips as Quincy waved his right hand left to right across his chest, never taking his piercing eyes off Milton. Suddenly, Lynton felt Milton jerk straight around, and as he stared into Quincy's eyes he murmured, "It is done."

Lynton held Milton in her grip, clinging to him with affection. Then, she realized what she was holding. It was Milton's lifeless body. Life had gone from him. Quincy had stolen his soul.

THE END

Don't Miss These Lynton Adventures
by
J. Wayne Frye

Lynton Curls Her Hair

----

*Lynton Buys A New Cell Phone
and Hears the Voice of Doom*

Lynton Walks on Water

Lynton and the Vampire at Tagaytay Manor

----

*Lynton Viñas and Beowulf Perez:
Demon Slayers in the Taal Inferno*

www.ingramcontent.com/pod-product-compliance
Lightning Source LLC
Chambersburg PA
CBHW070846120626
46556CB00002B/893